# PARANOIA

# PARANOIA

## *Craig DiLouie*

SALVO PRESS
Bend, Oregon

PARANOIA

Copyright © 2002 by Craig DiLouie

Salvo Press
P.O. Box 9095
Bend, OR 97708
www.salvopress.com


Library of Congress Control Number: 2001091242

ISBN: 1-930486-30-8

Printed in U.S.A
First Edition

## Acknowledgements

Several people and books helped make *Paranoia* possible and deserve my recognition and gratitude: Christine, my hilarious, beautiful and supportive wife; Randy, my friend and personal editor throughout all the years I've been pounding on keyboards; Guy, who introduced me to the world of conspiracy theories; my brother Chris, who is a great sounding board for the weird ideas I throw at him for novels; my mom, of course; *UFOs, JFK and Elvis* by Richard Belzer; *Rule of Secrecy* by Jim Marrs; *Conspiranoia! The Mother of All Conspiracy Theories* by Devon Jackson; *The 70 Greatest Conspiracies of All Time* by Jonathan Vankin and John Whalen; and ParaScope.com, Disinfo.com, WhatreallyHappened.com and the many other web sites that deal with the world of conspiracy theories. See more at: www.GrandConspiracy.com.

*"It is useless to deny, because it is impossible to conceal, that a great part of Europe—the whole of Italy and France and a great portion of Germany, to say nothing of other countries—is covered with a network of...secret societies.... They do not want constitutional government...they want to change the tenure of land, to drive out the present owners of the soil and to put an end to ecclesiastical establishments."*

—British Prime Minister Benjamin Disraeli, addressing the House of Commons, 1856


*"Some of the biggest men in the United States, in the field of commerce and manufacture, are afraid of somebody, are afraid of something. They know there is a power somewhere so organized, so subtle, so watchful, so interlocked, so complete, so pervasive that they had better not speak above their breath when they speak in condemnation of it."*

—President Woodrow Wilson, *The New Freedom*, 1913


*"The truth of the matter is, as you and I know, that a financial element in the large centers has owned the government ever since the days of Andrew Jackson."*

—President Franklin D. Roosevelt, in a letter to Woodrow Wilson's top adviser, Colonel Edward House, 1933


*"The USA is not run by its would-be 'democratic government.' Nothing could be more pathetic than the role that has to be played by the President of the United States, whose power is approximately zero."*

—R. Buckminster Fuller, 1986


*"There is just enough sanity in some of these conspiracy theories to make them almost believable. By and large, however, they are creations of very rich imaginations because we simply can't accept life as it is."*

—Ray Brown, Bowling Green University Professor

# Part One

# 1

Emmet Galt is possibly one of two people and I have to kill both of them.

*You should be lying in the bushes about seventy-five yards from the front door.*

In one reality, Galt is a recluse billionaire—an eccentric, harmless bachelor who loves dogs and generously donates millions to charities and the arts each year.

*Do not hesitate. Shoot him in the head. If you get a follow-up tap to the chest, good.*

In another reality, Galt is the most powerful man in the world and leads a secret society that has been at war with the Catholic Church for nearly two thousand years.

This secret society is called the Illuminati. You can find them in almost any book on conspiracy theories at your local bookstore. What makes them truly secret is that almost nobody believes these books.

*Remember your training.*

The front lawn of Emmet Galt's house is lit up like a football stadium and crawling with men in black. Any minute now, the old man himself is going to come out and walk straight into the crosshairs of the scope of my Zeuge-78 high-powered sniper rifle.

*He should be coming out in less than ten minutes.*

Chafing in my black insulated jumper, I clench my teeth and sigh through my nose. I just want this over with.

Galt and I have one thing in common. Both of us are one of two people depending on what you believe. In one reality, I'm an unemployed mental health worker, your average nobody who gets a gun and goes postal. In another, I'm mankind's last hope.

Basically, if you believe one thing, then he's the nut, and if you believe the other, then I'm the nut. The truth is so obscure, I don't even know which reality is right. You might say I'm the nut but then I'd say, well, you really don't know for sure, do you.

Reality, I've learned in the past seven days, is definitely how you look at it. That means that certain kinds of information can be considered a virus, and once it infects you, it changes one little bit of your worldview, then another, until your entire world shifts. If it shifts too much or shifts too fast, then you're not sure what reality is anymore.

Based on this, one could say that any profound revelation causes a detachment from reality.

*Remember not to hesitate. Simply exhale, hold it, size up your target and squeeze the trigger. The act itself has no significance. It is just an act. Like tying your shoelaces.*

I lay on the cold grass with my shoulder stiff and numb against the stock of the rifle, the barrel of which is resting on a bipod. It's pitch black where I'm hiding outside the wide semi-circle of light in front of the house, and I have a clean shot at the front door.

This part, what I'm seeing and doing right now, is all too true.

The Zeuge-78 is about four feet long, even longer with the silencer threaded onto the barrel. It weighs about ten pounds. It has a fiberglass stock with a one-inch decelerator pad and an ergonomic design. The cheekpiece is adjustable. The trigger is a standard Remington trigger retuned by German engineers. Trigger pressure is set at two and a half pounds.

I know all about guns because Palmer trained me.

*He should be coming out any minute now.*

That voice I keep hearing in my head is Palmer. My brother.

He's talking to me through an earpiece. He's back at the house, tracking me using global positioning satellites.

*Remember, Chad, if you pull the trigger, you will save the world.*

I guess by now you're thinking that I'm the nut, but this was all his idea.

*Good luck!*

The problem is that in less than three hours, the power is going to be cut across the entire eastern United States for twelve hours, causing chaos, an experiment to see how well the government can enact emergency powers. Then an Army-brewed germ is going to be sprayed on cities around the world, killing, well, almost everybody. After that, Galt and his people will come out of their bunkers and create a dictatorship of the enlightened.

If I shoot Galt, and the other assassins kill the rest of the Masters of the Illuminati at about the same time, then there will be nobody to push the button and the world will be saved.

Or so the theory goes.

The problem is if that if I kill him, then all these terrible things will be prevented but basically life will go on as before. If we win, nothing will happen.

Imagine global warming suddenly not happening anymore. Imagine that we're able to prevent it. You'd never really know for sure, would you.

This is what happens when you kill a theory.

The problem is I don't know anything for sure. Anything. And yet I'm here with a rifle that some Jesuit priests gave me, aiming it at a door and in a minute, less than a minute, I'm going to kill some old guy I don't even know.

People have already died.

In case you're thinking that I'm happy about any of this, I'm not. Just a week ago, I didn't go in for anything like this. I had to be convinced.

It's cold here lying on Galt's lawn and my blood is freezing in my veins. My stomach does a sudden dive. I'm thinking, there's no such thing as the Illuminati. It's all a paranoid fantasy. I'm thinking, Palmer's a nut, and he's turned me into one, too.

He seems to know what I'm thinking because I hear his voice in my ear.

*What if there is no God or a Heaven, says the atheist.*

*What if you die and find out there is a God and a Heaven, says the Christian.*

*The atheist converts.*

The front door of the house opens.

# 2

Rewind thirteen days.

Kevin is a whale of a man, a great white whale, and I'm chained to him like Captain Ahab, going down. We fall to the floor in a heap, Kevin and me and Martin Dobbs and Ray Barnes, panting and sliding around.

Mental health orderlies get taught the same thing that cops do, that people are damn hard to take down and just as hard to keep down. People are, well, slippery.

Kevin's problem is that he's a paranoid schizophrenic and right now, he's getting wild.

In the profession, we call this "acting out."

Most times, a patient acts out and they flail around, but they're not trying to hurt you, they're just freaking out. If you stay out of their way and get behind them, you can restrain them long enough to get them into the pink room, slap a helmet on them and wait it out.

Kevin, on the other hand, believes that we're trying to drag him to a gas chamber. In his mind, he's fighting for his life.

Mercer County Psychiatric is your basic public mental hospital just outside of Trenton, New Jersey. It has one hundred and twenty beds for inpatients and treats adults aged eighteen and over. Some hospitals, the private ones, are like hotels and treat everything, including eating disorders, compulsive gambling and sex addiction.

Our hospital, well, it's not that fancy.

Mostly, we get your cookie cutter nuts with mental and behavioral disorders, and we have a large population of drug addicts. We don't have an outpatient program. We treat them and if they can function well enough to leave, we put them back on the street.

We orderlies never say, "Goodbye." We always say, "See you later."

Most of the time, they wind up back at the hospital.

We try to make it nice, though. Our doctors have caught on to the whole holistic healing concept, recognizing that every human being has a "mind, body, emotions and soul," and that the entire person must be treated. We even have a small arts program.

Everything about the place, from its gray walls to the ancient TV sets mounted up high around the ceiling to the crummy carpet that is literally right out of the 1970s, tells you that while the place tries to be fancy, it is anything but. In fact, I think the harder the hospital tries, the more you realize what it's lacking.

To me, however, it is as familiar as home. It's where I work.

Kevin's face is purple and he's not screaming anymore. The room is quiet except for four men grunting and the scuffle of sneakers and Dobbs talking quietly as he holds on to the whale. Kevin's sweating a river, which makes it hard for me to keep a hold on him. My nose is pressed against his wet fat arm, where there's a tattoo of a grinning, flaming skull.

My job is to help the nurses and doctors treat the patients, and to help the patients take care of themselves, do what they're told and not beat up or rape each other. To do your job the right way, you use a combination of good cop, bad cop, but both have to come from you.

Right now, we're being bad cops. We're sliding around on the floor trying to get a hold on Kevin and keep him down long enough to take a shot of sedative.

Dobbs, however, is trying to soothe Kevin, telling him everything is going to be all right and that we're here to help him. He offers to sit down with Kevin and talk it out, for hours, if that's what he wants. But he must be quiet first. He must relax and let us help him.

The thing about Dobbs is, he means it. He has a good heart.

Kevin screams at Dobbs surprisingly loud, his lungs blasting like the twin barrels of shotguns, exploding at his mouth, spraying spittle across the floor.

He accuses Dobbs of putting a chip in his head so that the government could read his mind and control his thoughts, and now, because he knows too much, he is going to be murdered.

That's why I keep quiet during moments like this. I don't get involved with the patients anymore, because you can never win. I once quizzed a guy who thought he was Jesus Christ about the Bible and asked him, if he really was Jesus, why he got the answers wrong.

"You've got the wrong Bible," said the nut.

I told Dobbs about it and he didn't think it was as funny as I did. And he told me that mental health professionals don't use the word, "nut."

Finally, mercifully, the nurse comes and gets a shot into Kevin, and after a few moments, the whale relaxes in my grip.

"You okay, Kevin?" Dobbs says. "You're not hurt, are you?"

Kevin, loaded up with sedative, answers dreamily that it's good to feel pain. He says that if man didn't feel pain, he'd eat himself.

•

All people in the world want three things and will do or believe anything to achieve them:

To exist. That means being noticed, feeling loved, and not feeling alone.

To procreate with the right person (women) or as many people as possible (men).

To live forever.

Most nuttiness has to do with these three basic needs.

The problem with our species is that consciousness was a byproduct of our evolution. Mind and body are always warring with each other. Rationalization was invented so that these two creatures could get along.

People like to see themselves as part of this majority population that is normal in terms of looks and sanity. Us. The oddballs are this little slice of humanity that is too fat, too ugly or outright nuts. They let you know right away that they're nuts by, you know, drooling, talking back at the voices in their head, acting out or finding it interesting to watch paint dry for hours. Accidents, you might call them. A well-defined population. Them. What most people don't understand, however, is that it's not so cut and dried. We're all in the same pot. The human race is constantly evolving. I'm a real biology freak, almost as much as I am about psychology. Anyway, you'd think that mutations only give people major problems like schizophrenia and cancer, but they also result in big noses, attached earlobes and every type of personality and nuttiness imaginable spread out over a broad spectrum.

Just look at the Internet. Or your average Jerry Springer show. Or New York City.

Just about all of us are nuts at one point or another, when you get right down to it. Thanks to evolution, all of us are mutants.

Take your run-of-the-mill Christian, for example. He goes to church and believes that when he dies, he will go to Heaven and live forever in a state of bliss. Then he says he never read the Bible and could care less about religion. In fact, he's embarrassed to even talk about it.

Try to tell me that's sane behavior.

Most of us occasionally get the urge to stuff merchandise inside our jackets at the department store, punch some stranger whose face we don't like, grab a girl's ass on the street, or yank on the wheel and pull our cars into oncoming traffic. A lot of people throw salt over their shoulder or won't walk under a ladder. Other people won't use public restrooms because they think they'll get

VD from the toilet seat. Some people are drop-dead terrified of spiders, others of public speaking or dropping babies or going outdoors. Some people, when somebody calls them and hangs up, check to make sure all their doors are locked. A lot of people, you put them on top of the world's tallest building and they have to fight the urge to jump. Some killed themselves when the *War of the Worlds* program was broadcast, others when the year 2000 came with all its Y2K end-of-the-world paranoia. Millions of them believe that angels are intervening all their time in their lives. Millions give money to TV evangelists, speak in tongues or pierce them, join cults, believe in management techniques such as quality circles and sensitivity training, drink their own piss for the health benefit, generalize about and fear people of other races, and—in an irony that only humans are capable of—like to punish anybody who's "different."

These people are not in mental institutions. They drive cabs, operate on brains, run the government, design new products, fly commercial airplanes, cook your food in restaurants.

Everybody is crazy at times, especially, it seems, when it comes to the emotions of worry and hope.

Knowing this, I learned long ago not to judge.

I also keep a loaded gun in the house, just in case.

•

Dr. Hiram Gaines, a gnomish middle-aged man wearing large black glasses and wrinkled tie, shirt and pants, is our hospital's biggest paranoid schizophrenic, but unlike Kevin, he never gets violent. Out in the world, he's a conspiracy guru and the author of *Conspiracies Refound*, a classic in the field, I'm told. Rumor also had it that before his decline off the deep end, he'd been a psychologist. In my experience, psychologists make the biggest nuts. You may have heard that the reason a lot of people become psychologists is because they're completely messed up and want to find out what's wrong with themselves. Or maybe it's because screwed-up people have a need to fix everybody else.

You don't enter Gaines' room; you are confronted with it. In there, you leave the safety of the hospital and enter a reflection of the wacky world that's inside his head. The shades are drawn and the small lamps produce a dim light that only contributes to the gloom. The air is thick and stuffy and smells like an unventilated smoking room at the world's oldest hotel.

And the walls, ceiling, desk—every conceivable surface—are all covered with newspaper clippings and drawings that look like organizational charts and flowcharts.

Thanks to his illness, Gaines has, well, an active imagination. While he chainsmokes unfiltered Camels in the middle of the hospital's biggest fire hazard, he looks for and explains connections between even the tiniest of world events. He would make a good chaos theorist, proving that an actual butterfly flapping its wings in Peking really did cause a tornado in Wyoming. He'd be able to name the butterfly responsible and point it out at a lineup.

Many was the time he tried to explain to me, in that raving monotone of his, how every clipping on the wall was connected to every other clipping, and how the cohesive whole, always growing until even parts of the ceiling were covered, was the mother of all conspiracies.

Gaines likes to say, "Don't be afraid of conspiracy theories, Mr. Carver. Conspiracies are nothing new. Even Adam and Eve conspired to eat the apple from the Tree of Knowledge and hide it from God. Conspiracy was one of the first things humans did."

Millions of people in America believe in conspiracy theories, many more than you would imagine. Gaines has sold something like a million copies of his book.

Some of the doctors I work with told me that conspiracy theories help off-balance people make sense of a chaotic world. Fine, I say, but I think there's something more. There's the cheap thrill.

This is how urban legends start.

Somebody tells a weird story and it takes off and gets around the country in a massive game of telephone, a process that's accelerated by the Internet. Even though you know it's bullshit, you want to believe it because it gives you this thrill. You're learning secrets and seeing evil and this is exciting to you. The snowball keeps rolling; eventually, it builds mass and becomes truth. Some company's soft drink gets accused of causing impotence, and even though the charge is proven false by the FDA and this is stated in the press, nobody wants to drink it. A story comes out about a baby dying in some ugly experiment decades ago, and a hundred web sites later the story now includes a thousand black babies being thrown into a bonfire by the U.S. Army.

Whether you believe in UFOs, angels, ghosts, Satan, lost civilizations or conspiracies, it all comes from the same part of the brain that craves mystery, secrets, problem-solving and a cheap thrill. Then you go back to your boring or terrible life and long for more of that thrill, that cheap escape from the real world.

For some people, the fantasy world takes over and becomes reality. It happens by degrees, by seduction, by self-brainwashing. The process is really quite simple.

Conspiracies are the bed where reality and fantasy sleep together. They're the line between the real and the surreal, the layer of icing on the American fruitcake.

People will step over that thin line and believe just about anything because they want to. Because it's fun for them to do so. The illusion, the danger and the mystery are all part of the fun. It's like going into a haunted house. Or taking a rollercoaster ride.

Today, Gaines is excited.

"There is a rift," he says enigmatically, dragging heavily on his Camel.

"That's great, Doc."

I hate when people are condescending, especially if I'm the one doing it, but I'm sick of hearing about this stuff. Some conspiracy theorists are fanatics who live for their theories. They're kind of like born-again Christians, except with Christians you get a good payoff: You go to Heaven. For conspiracy theorists, the payoff is the bad guys take over the world and throw all the nice people in a gas chamber. There's never closure, and it's depressing.

"There is a rift in the Invisible Empire," he explains. "I sense hesitation. And something more. The beginning of three final calamitous events that will fulfill the Plan."

"Bad things happen in threes," I tell him, grateful for the opportunity to say something relevant in a conversation I otherwise can't follow.

"Fives," he corrects me, eyeing me through his thick glasses.

"So we already had two bad things happen?"

Gaines grunts like a disgusted teacher.

"I've only been explaining them to you over the past two months. In painstaking detail."

"Oh, right." I hand him a stack of newspapers. "Here's your papers, Doc."

His eyes light up as he accepts them gingerly. "Ah, yes, thank you."

Conspiracy theorists are also like addicts. Information is their drug and they'll do anything to get more.

He glances at the front page of *The New York Times*, looks up in amazement, then shows me a headline about President Jackson announcing that he will pay off the national debt.

"See this?"

"Yeah, we're finally paying off the debt. It's great stuff."

"No, it's not great stuff. Wake up, Mr. Carver!"

"Come on, Doc, give me a break today."

"It's coming soon. The last pieces of the puzzle are falling into place. The Invisible Empire will fulfill its Plan, and we will be their slaves. Those of us lucky to survive the last three events, that is. This is the catalyst for the third event. Somebody important is going to die. The man in our highest office. I've finally cracked it!"

"Good, Doc. I'm happy for you."

Gaines glares at me, chewing on his beard.

"Don't be happy for me," he says. "It's you I'm worried about, Mr. Carver."

I think I'm immune to weirdness after twelve years in this

place, but I confess that the man honestly gives me that queasy feeling I get when I ignore an e-mailed chain letter.

He says, "Something terrible is about to happen. It's about time you woke up."

# 3

I'm sitting in my kitchen, staring at the handgun on the table in front of me, and I'm telling myself that I'm not really going to kill my wife. Not really.

I want to, see, but I won't do it.

For one, I could never hurt her, no matter what she did to me.

There's also the little problem of me not knowing where she is.

In any case, I am boiling rage made manifest.

It's times like this when you really understand the expression, "I was beside myself." It's like you're outside of your own body, watching yourself explode into fury, and you have no idea who this raging lunatic is. It's only later that you get perspective, when you look back, except that by then you're trying as hard as you can to forget it ever happened.

Six hours ago, I drove home still haunted by that queasy gut-wrench Gaines had given me. He's a regular Hannibal Lecter the way he gets inside your head. He leaves you with that feeling you get all day after a bad dream the night before. You can't shake it.

Something terrible is about to happen, he said.

It's you I'm worried about, he said.

I come home to an empty house and find the note on my refrigerator.

In the note, my wife, Jenny, tells me that she's leaving me for another man and that they ran off together. Goodbye.

Shit! Fuck!

I'm ashamed to admit it, but my next emotion was, well, a kind of relief. I was titillated, imagining endless miles of privacy, other women, new potentials, a little peace and quiet.

For the past two years or so, see, I actually wished that she would simply disappear.

I wished, for example, that she would not be there pacing the kitchen talking on the phone to her friends all the time, so loud that I could never really watch TV in the living room without constantly feeling distracted and irritated. I wished that she wouldn't nag me to take her someplace fun, usually a girlie movie or ice skating, of all things.

Like the other women who have come and gone in my life, my mother being the first, Jenny always wanted it both ways.

She wanted me mysterious and aloof, but also sensitive and doting. She wanted me outgoing, but not around other people. She wanted me to be her personal Don Juan who would simultaneously conquer her and be conquered by her, reappearing as a new Don Juan every day.

Jenny wanted it both ways all the time, and I had to be two people.

She would make herself things, then say, "I wish you had given me this." She would lose things all the time, then if I didn't help her find them she would get mad. Then there's the fact that she was constantly criticizing me and trying to improve me.

It was, you know, a marriage.

After a while, I got tired. I had already been tired, which is one reason why I settled down with her in the first place.

Anyhow, I get this note on my refrigerator and that's all I get after ten years of marriage. She didn't even tell me who the guy is. Five minutes later, my elation was gone, replaced by rage and depression and denial and acceptance, which proceeded to cycle every two hours in an endless loop right up until the present moment in the night's darkest hours. It's like I have to gulp down the truth every two hours, then retch it back up, like some guy in a Greek myth. I do everything I can not to picture her running off with some guy I know, but I end up picturing her sleeping with every one of my friends.

In any case, I wanted her gone. Now she's gone, and I realize I hate my life.

I also settled down with her, and stayed with her, because I love her.

It was, you know, a marriage.

Talk about wanting it both ways.

•

The next day I call in sick, then the next. I call in sick for four days in a row.

"It's getting to you, huh?" Martin Dobbs, my boss, says after the fourth time.

He means my job. My job must be getting to me, he is saying. He has no idea that my wife left me because she found another man more satisfying. Another man I don't know, who could be anybody—one of my closest friends, the guy who rings up our groceries, a total stranger—anybody. Which makes him every-body.

In fact, right now, I'm picturing Dobbs having sex with her.

I grip the phone with a sweaty hand. I'm holding my gun with the other.

"No," I tell him. "I'm just sick. In the stomach."

I'm not lying to him. At this moment, my stomach is in a dou-ble-knot.

"All right," he says in his gravelly voice, trying not to be patronizing.

He seems to know, to have figured out using his professional intuition, that I'm on the edge. We work at a mental institution, and everybody gets unstable after a while unless they become and stay totally detached. Even then, cracks may appear at any time. We learn how to tell if somebody is becoming unhinged just by the tone of their voice. He's probably thinking that the wrestling match with Kevin was the straw that snapped this camel's back.

I know this and think I'm faking it well, but I'm like the drunk who's trying to sound sober in front of the cop.

"Really," I tell him, drenched in sweat. "I'm fine. Just one more day. Then I'll see you on Monday."

"Take care of yourself," says Dobbs, who has a good heart. "Call me if you need to."

"I'm fine," I say, and hang up.

I decide that I'm going to kill myself.

On an impulse, I push the barrel against my temple and close my eyes tight.

Squeeze, don't pull. That's how you're supposed to fire a gun. Instant relief. Problem solved. This will show her.

Then I think better of it.

I'm thinking, what if you don't automatically go to Heaven. What if you blow your brains out and that's it. Oblivion. That gets me really depressed, but it does make me realize that things could be worse. Sudden death awareness is like pounding a fresh cup of coffee. You're not meant to have it until you're old.

The truth is, I don't know what I'm going to do. The bad part is I'm mad at the world and I've been carrying a loaded handgun around the house, wondering which phase—anger, depression, denial, acceptance—will be the one where I'll need it.

I bought that gun, ironically, because everybody is not what they seem. You can talk to somebody for hours and you think they're charming and brilliant, and the next thing you know they're telling you that they were once kidnapped by aliens.

Let's just say the mass murderers of the world, well, they're often the nice, quiet type.

If everybody is nutty to some degree, you've got to protect yourself against the unknown.

Also consider that your best friend who's grinning and shaking your hand might be screwing your wife behind your back, planning their escape from you.

I open the closet door, pull down the shoebox, and put the gun

back. That's the first rational thing I'm able to do after finding
out that she'd gone, and it gives me hope.

Then I roam the house for the rest of the day, shooting off
philosophical gunfire, asking myself the same questions between
quiet bouts of self-pity.

How do you really know anybody? How do you know if you
can trust them? How do you believe anything they say if ten years
or even ten minutes later they don't believe it themselves?

I need a great big cry to let some of this out, but I can't do it
yet. I have to find the right phrase, like, "I'll never see her again,"
or, "Next week is our anniversary."

The doorbell rings and I run to answer it, thinking maybe it's
Jenny. Maybe she saw her mistake and decided to come home.

My heart pounds and my stomach flips as I race down the
stairs.

Of course, Jenny has a house key and wouldn't ring the bell.
She would just let herself in. A part of me knows that but can't
fight the nuttiness of hope. I keep running.

I open the door and it's my brother Palmer, standing there. The
sun is setting behind him, its light orange and golden, creating a
play of fire on his blond hair.

"Hey, Chad."

I don't say anything, struck speechless, my mouth hanging
open.

He barges past me carrying these suitcases, his eyes wild and
his long hair streaming behind him.

I haven't seen my brother in fifteen years, since we were kids,
since he ran away from home and disappeared without a trace.
Talk about weird timing.

It's the best time for him to show up, and the worst time.

•

I live in Riverdale, a place that has just over five thousand people in it, which barely qualifies it as a city. Nestled on the
Delaware River, it's your average nice small town and a place
that time and history has swept by and left behind. People know

each other by name in that town, and they wave at you or give a polite little honk when they drive by in their cars. I'm not kidding. It's set up on a grid, but the houses are old, and the town has its own history. Not far from Riverdale is the spot where George Washington crossed the Delaware to attack the Hessians in New Jersey. A lot of trade was ferried across the river and up and down the canals in the 1800s; even today, the canal is still there and the tow paths with them, where the mules pulled the barges up and down the canal. The railroads came along after that, and Riverdale had its own train station, which is now a restaurant with a hotel attached for the tourists who come down from New York to hunt for antiques and detox in the quaint atmosphere and slow pace. A nice, quiet little town.

It's nice to know in this day and age that friendly, trusting towns like this one are still around. I plan to hold onto it for as long as possible.

Riverdale is where Palmer and I grew up, in this very house. When I was seventeen and he was fourteen, our parents died in a car crash. I joined the Air Force to make money so that I could take care of us.

My brother was always off in his own head. You look at our family photo album, and there are all these Polaroid shots of him as a little kid playing with his toys outside in the dirt, the pupils of his eyes red if a flash was used, not really there but somewhere else. He lived in a world of the imagination. As he got older, he was that skinny weird kid that the jocks picked on, but he didn't seem to mind it, always smiling. His smile was full of secrets.

He got straight As without studying. Instead of picking on him, although he was smarter than me, the older brother, I admired him for that. I'm smart in my own right. But my smarts are more of the type required when you're going to rewire your own house without any training. I just know how to do stuff like that. Palmer, though, lived in another world. He read books all the time, made drawings, wrote stories.

I still have some of them up in a box in the attic.

Palmer had always needed attention and when Mom and Dad died, he needed it all the more. Therapy for him, I guess. My life revolved around him. That was therapy for me, too. The problem was, he never gave you his attention back. We fought a lot because of that, but we depended on each other.

The strange thing is that after our parents died, Palmer changed at school for the better. He dressed better, took a girl to the prom, joined the wrestling team, became a normal person. But I still couldn't get inside his head, really get to know him. I always had this weird sense, call it intuition, that he was faking being normal.

When I turned nineteen and Palmer was sixteen, he ran away from home after his junior prom without a word, a note, anything, just some empty drawers and closets.

Fifteen years ago.

I'm asking myself, how do you really know anybody, even your own brother.

I envied Palmer for splitting even while I was stunned with massive rejection. When you grow up in a small town and you're that young, you hate living there and all you can think about is how great it'd be to drop everything and leave, go somewhere, anywhere.

Not anymore, though. When you reach your thirties as I have, you tend to want to go home. That small town seems safe to you. Comfortable. Not too good, not too bad: Just right.

After Palmer ran away, Jenny filled the void.

I still had a compulsive need to take care of everything and everybody, and Jenny wanted me to take care of her.

Because of this, I never did go to college. Jenny wanted to get married when I got out of the Air Force, and I couldn't support her, keep the house and go to school. So I got a job.

Now she dumped me and took off without a trace, just like Palmer did all those years ago, leaving me stunned and recovering, stationary while the ones I loved kept leaving.

I have lived my life, making choices that were my own but were also, in a sense, made for me.

•

Palmer marches up the stairs, his hands and arms filled with
suitcases. He seems to know the house and where the spare bed-
room is. I follow after him, my mouth still hanging open, while
he flops the suitcases onto the bed and starts unpacking.

"Make yourself at home, Palmer," I manage to say, studying
him with my arms crossed.

He pauses and glances at me, his wild expression telling me
that he's in some sort of trouble, while also telling me to forget it
and not ask any questions. He is carrying a huge burden, I can
tell. His eyes are practically begging me to make him spill his
guts. I know that desperate look well.

Instead, he says, "I'm sorry that your wife left you, Chad."

"How did you know that? In fact, how did you even know
where I live, Jesus?"

I used to call him Jesus when we were kids when I felt like
busting his balls. It is actually Palmer's middle name, as in:
Palmer Jesus Carver.

"It's a small town," he says. "Everybody knows your business.
Riverdale hasn't changed a bit since I left. It's funny how everybody's worried about the Internet stealing your privacy, as if you
had any to begin with."

"What the hell happened to you?"

He opens some drawers and starts putting away stacks of neat-
ly folded underwear, shaking his head.

"No, I can't. Listen. I don't want to get you involved."

I don't like his tone. Like I said, you don't work at a mental
hospital without learning a lot about a man's mental condition
simply from the sound of his voice.

"Oh no you don't—"

"Listen, Chad," he says quietly, which makes me shut up and
listen. "Me being here doesn't make you involved. Don't worry
about that. But they know what I say all the time. I'm being
watched, listened to, recorded. Now, probably. Definitely. So I
can be here, but if I tell you anything, then you'll be involved and

we both don't want that."

"Don't even start pulling that psychological crap on me. If you don't want to get somebody involved, you don't tell him, 'I don't want to get you involved.' You simply don't involve him. And you definitely don't try to make him curious so he pries it out of you."

He hangs his shirts up in the closet.

I say, "I'm not sitting here dying to know what happened to you, Palmer. After the week I've just had, I don't want to know. Actually, it's important for you to know that I lived my life for the past fifteen years and they didn't revolve around you."

It's like we're teenagers again, having the same old arguments.

I thought I was over the anger and betrayal I felt when be ran away fifteen years ago, but I'm not. I'm so angry, in fact, that I don't care right now why he left.

Besides, I'm still in a rage over my wife, and Palmer is the perfect target.

He opens another suitcase. This one doesn't have clothes in it. It's loaded with a jumble of strange electronic gear.

My curiosity gets the better of me and I forget for a minute that I'm pissed.

"What have you got there, Palmer?"

He holds up a small hand-held box.

"This is an audio jammer. I hope the batteries are still good."

He clicks it on, checks it and, apparently satisfied that it works, puts it on the dresser.

"Oh shit," I say, feeling a sense of foreboding.

Audio jammers, Palmer says, protect your privacy. They jam bugs, hard-wired mikes, shotgun/parabolic mikes, laser bounce listening devices and your standard tape recorder. We could have a conversation anywhere within one hundred and fifty feet, he says, and not even a Company spook could listen to your conversation unless he was right there.

"Uh-huh," I say, not knowing what else to say, my mind occupied with the irony of my brother possibly being a nut. Things go full circle, don't they.

"Now we can talk freely," he adds. "But I still don't want to get you involved."

"Okay," I tell him. No problem.

For a second there, at that first moment when I saw him as I opened the door, I was happy. I thought, here's my long-lost brother, my own flesh and blood, tramping home like the prodigal son. His timing is perfect. I can talk to him and he will understand and help me.

Instead, now I have a feeling I'm going to have to help him.

And with that thought, my rage evaporates. I stare at him, confused, unable to act.

He shows me more of his collection. The next device looks like a Sony Walkman wired to a metal wand with a handgrip.

This transmitter detector is your basic bug sweeper, he says. It can find body wires, bumpers, transmitters and tracking devices. Wave this wand around and it makes a noise like a Geiger counter, except it squeals when you find a transmitter.

You can detect any source of RF with this, including carrier current transmitters, infrared and video cameras.

These headphones, he explains, are so that whoever's recording you doesn't hear the tell-tale noise and know you're doing a sweep.

I want to tell him to shut up, but I don't say anything. I feel like my great big cry might be coming on.

My trigger phrase might be, "My wife left me and now my brother's nuts."

He holds up another device.

This is an electronic sound amplifier with a booster mike and a parabolic dish. Some people use it for bird watching and for hunting. Others use it to conduct audio surveillance of a stationary or mobility-limited human target.

This is an LCD voltage meter that allows you to check the conditions of your phone line and determine if it has a tap on it or a bug in it.

This is an electric pick gun, and with it you can pick almost any lock.

This is a smoke detector with an occupancy sensor that triggers a hidden microvideocamera that was built into it.

You can buy knock-off versions of most of this stuff right off the Internet, he says, but it would cost you a small fortune. The devices he has are military-grade, the real thing.

I shrug. I wouldn't know the difference.

I swallow hard and ask him, "What the hell do you need all this stuff for, Palmer?"

He smiles. "The things I'm mixed up with . . . You wouldn't believe me, Chad."

"All right," I say. No problem.

He adds quietly, "Nobody would."

My rage returns. I roll my eyes and stomp out.

And I remember why Palmer and I hadn't gotten along that well back when we were kids. Our parents died and I was forced to be the adult, always thinking about practical things. Palmer was always in his own little world, and nobody else mattered.

He calls after me, telling me that I'm missing the really good stuff.

These are sunglasses that allow you to see behind you as well as forward.

This is a taser. It fires probes that attach to your target and send high voltages into his body, incapacitating him.

Now, it seems, his world has gotten the better of him. Palmer is obviously nuts.

Me, I keep thinking that everybody I thought I knew has turned into somebody else.

# 4

It's nighttime and Palmer and I are drinking beers in the dark and watching the Dolphins lose to the Redskins on my big-screen TV. Under normal circumstances, this would be a good thing, but tonight the house seems big and empty without Jenny filling it.

My brother is doing little to fill the space. His presence is like that little stone in your shoe you can't rid of. I can feel his neediness emanating from him in waves. I still can't tell if he is going to help nurse me back to health or drag me down.

My wife left me after ten years of marriage and my brother came home after fifteen years of being who knows where on the journey of his long, doomed orbit. There's a strange synchronism at work here, but my brain can't pursue it. It's hard to think straight when you're drunk and you've been crushed.

During halftime, Palmer gets up and leaves, then comes back just before the end of the game. He tells me that he debugged the house. We're clean, he says. He hands me another beer, then cracks open his own and sinks into the couch with a sigh.

In time, he says, he will tell me about the Masters of the World. When I am ready.

When the Redskins score the winning touchdown, I don't even yell.

•

"God, I miss her," I tell Palmer. We're sitting out on the porch, huddled in our jackets, drinking our beers. The street outside my house, Union Street, is empty. Across the street is a little league baseball field, also empty and dark. Most people are home sleeping at this time. It's pushing one in the morning, that time of night when I feel need and hunger. And it's cold, October cold.

When I wake up every day, I don't actually miss Jenny all that much, but by one in the morning, I'm dying for her. Late at night, while everybody else is asleep, a man can feel naked and helpless, sensing his own mortality in the lonesome dark. He starts his day like a lion but ends it like a lamb, needing the familiar warmth of his woman.

I say, "It's weird, but when I was with her all those years, I thought about other women all the time. Now I'm single, and I can't stand the idea of being with another woman."

Palmer grunts, telling me that he understands.

I say, "At the same time, a part of me wishes I had cheated on her when I had the chance. Then I wouldn't be hurting."

"Get them before they get you, right, Chad?"

"No," I say. "I don't really want that. What I had, I wasn't happy, but it was all I had."

"You can't make an omelet without breaking some eggs, then."

"What's that supposed to mean?"

Palmer shrugs. "You know. You'll come out all right. Look at the big picture. Your life isn't over. Every end is a beginning. Later, you'll be a better man. How is for you to decide."

"Yeah, I guess," I say, thinking, Palmer is starting to sound like a normal person.

"Me, I have to decide what I want to do now that I'm away from them."

Oh. That didn't last long.

"So who is them, anyhow?"

Palmer drinks his beer. "The Masters of the World, Chaderinski. The Puppet Masters."

He says this like I should know what he's talking about.

"Okay," I say. "And you carry all that electronic gear to help you fight them."

"Not to fight them." He snorts at my naïve-te. "Nobody can fight them. That stuff is for my protection."

"Palmer, is this some type of weird spy kick you're on, like when we were kids, or are you a conspiracy theorist run amok, or are you just plain crazy?"

"Given the choices, I guess I'd have to say I'm just plain crazy, Chad," he says dryly.

"I'm being serious. If you're going to live in my home and act like a nut I'd like to know what kind of nut you are. For my protection."

"All right, if you really want to know, I'm heavily involved in a plot to take over the United States by an ancient conspiracy of men who call themselves the Illuminati."

"That's enough," I say. "You've answered my question."

"That's right," Palmer says, irritated. "I'm crazy, as you can see."

"Playing reverse psychology will not make you credible to me."

"Then I can't win."

"Win what? What do you want from me?"

Palmer says, "I would like you to have an open mind, Chad."

"I thought you didn't want to get me involved."

"Well, suppose I know a friend of mine has less than a year to live. Do I not tell him, knowing that it will completely shatter him, or do I tell him, simply because he has a right to know?"

"It's not the same," I tell him.

"It's real. I was involved. Admit to yourself that you don't know what I've been doing all these years. You don't know what I've seen and know to be true. I don't expect you to believe me. I'm just wondering if you're open to possibilities without ridiculing me."

"I give up," I say. "Okay, I'm totally hooked. Tell me about what happened to you. Why don't you start with when you took off fifteen years ago without saying goodbye, all the way up to the present. Go ahead, tell me everything."

"Forget it, Chad. I've said too much already."

Palmer stares at his beer, blaming it.

"You're like a woman," I tell him, incredulous.

"Like I said, you won't believe me anyway. You'd think I was nuts."

"Worse than a woman."

"I'm sorry I left you like that, Chad. Without saying goodbye."

"Whatever."

"The President," he says with sudden venom, "will be shot and killed while doing a fundraiser in Chicago, three days from now."

I tell Palmer that he's a paranoid schizophrenic and needs medication.

That being said, I tell him good night, get up and go back into the house, heading for my big empty bed where I'll sleep alone and try not to picture Jenny with her new lover.

The President, Palmer shouts after me. On Monday, the President of the United States will be shot and killed. Then you will be ready to believe me.

As I climb into bed, just before I turn out the light, I put my gun under my pillow.

●

Nobody knows for sure what causes schizophrenia. It tends to run in the family (our Uncle Dave had it); some scientists believe that it's caused by a viral infection, bad nutrition during pregnancy, or complications while you're being born.

It is often confused with split-personality disorder, which is entirely different.

The problem is the brain has too much dopamine, a chemical that lets cells send messages to each other. As a result, you can't process external information like normal people. Bright lights and loud music in particular can send you into wild hallucinations.

Suddenly—sometime between the ages of fifteen and thirty-four, usually—you start to become confused, can't make decisions, withdraw from reality, stop taking care of yourself, suffer from delusions, argue a lot, become indifferent and, of course, hallucinate.

You might ask your friends why they are communicating with each other in a secret sign language, or suddenly believe they are reading your mind.

You might wake up with a headache and believe that scientists implanted a microchip in your head while you were sleeping.

You might hear loud scary voices that make fun of you, warn you of imagined danger or tell you what to do.

Schizophrenics see things that aren't there, hear voices that aren't there, feel things that aren't there, and believe things that aren't true. The bad ones have to be hospitalized. Sometimes, these bad ones have to be restrained and given electroconvulsive therapy.

More than two and a half million Americans are diagnosed schizophrenics.

Paranoid schizophrenics are a special breed. These are schizophrenics who are convinced that people are out to get them, and they suffer delusions of grandeur. They are at the center of vast intricate conspiracies.

The amazing thing about these people is how convincing they can be. They have an answer for everything. You can't trip them up. Some of them seem to talk faster than many people can think. Most of them are men, who invented the "answer for everything." Male DNA is wired so that you get more mutations, which means more geniuses but also many more nuts than among women. Most serial killers are men.

Paranoid schizophrenia is treatable with drugs like Thorazine, Risperdal and Haldol. These medications can make you tired, sick to your stomach and suffer other side effects. After that, therapy is used to relieve stress and help the victim become more aware of his disease and how to cope with it.

I've got a strong suspicion that my brother Palmer is a paranoid schizophrenic.

He told me about how they were recording, watching, listening to him. I'm willing to bet my life savings that they-these Illuminati people, Masters of the World, whatever—are some international cabal of Jewish bankers or somesuch nonsense, and he is at the center of a big conspiracy that, if you itemize the resources and technology required, is right now costing said international cabal hundreds of millions of dollars along with a litter of bodies to cover its tracks. Just keeping him under surveillance is probably costing a million a day.

He also doesn't trust me, but the more skeptical I am of him the more he will. He will need to convince me. The best thing for me to do, I know, is to treat him as I treated Jenny: Be skeptical but in the end say you're right, I agree with you, thanks.

All his fancy spy gadgets do not impress me. They do not give him any credibility. Actually, they're another clue that he has a diseased mind. Paranoid schizophrenics really love electronics and automation. It's a big turn-on for them. I'm waiting for him to tell me about the other electronic devices I haven't seen yet, the ones implanted in his head, ass, whatever.

The sad thing about paranoid schizophrenia for friends and family of the victim is that they see their friend or whatever show up one day as a different person. In this case, Palmer Jesus Carver is no longer my brother, this guy I grew up with. He is no longer a person, from one point of view. He is a machine with a tape recorder in his head that will be set in an endless loop repeating his theories about how the world is out to get him.

I haven't heard the theories yet, but they're coming. I've seen a thousand guys just like Palmer go in and out of Mercer County Psychiatric. He's got all the signs.

And I'm stuck with him, it seems.

It's pretty bad if you have to take care of one of these people, but it could be worse. Through no fault of your own, you could suddenly become a paranoid schizophrenic yourself. Then one day you'll hear screaming in your head telling you to kill the gas station attendant because, as the voices tell you, he is filling your tank with nitroglycerine.

So I guess that makes me lucky.

It's a good thing I've got experience with these people, or else I would get suckered in for a long hard ride. This is because at first, you listen to the paranoid schizophrenic and you almost believe him. I mean, the conspiracies are always elaborate and this is your friend talking, a friend you think is sane. Then you question him about his conspiracies and he has an answer for everything, and that answer is always elaborate and convincing. You can ask questions and see the answers, formulated on the spot with a certain genius, add incredible layers of complexity to what is already a complex conspiracy. Once formulated, these answers become cardinal truth and are stored in memory. Because of this, you almost believe him.

The whole thing also turns you on. A part of you actually wants it to be real. It's pretty amazing. Nuttiness is contagious.

Where the schizophrenic slips up is that the conspiracy always gets bigger and bigger, and that's all he can talk about. Talking and externalizing all the demons in his head, until he gets the right drugs, is his only relief from mental torture.

After a while, the conspiracy begins to involve entire nations, TV networks, satellites, CIA, FBI, Trilateral Commission, Mafia, Jewish bankers, Freemasons and other organizations all spending billions of dollars on their conspiracy to monitor, harass—and, in the future, assassinate—one insignificant person.

If he works for a telecommunications, media or a hi-tech company, it adds a whole other dimension, makes things even more interesting.

Me, I've heard it all before, believe me.

After a while, you get torn apart from loving your friend who's no longer there and being afraid of this insane person who at any moment might finger you as out to get him.

Some of these people are suicidal and worse, homicidal.

Palmer is a paranoid schizophrenic.

# 5

When Palmer and I were kids, I built a treehouse for him in the woods far back behind the elementary school. Palmer was eleven and I was fourteen at the time. We had some scrap wood left over from when our father built a doghouse for Achilles and Hector, our beagles. We both loved the dogs, although I was the one who had to take care of them. You couldn't even give Palmer goldfish; he'd find a way to kill them through sheer absent-minded neglect. Off in a dreamworld, he'd forget what day it was, where he left things, what chores he had to do around the house, so I was the one who had to brush the dogs after their baths, change their flea collars and clean their ears to prevent yeast infection. I didn't mind, though; taking care of the dogs was a way for me to love them. I also got to teach them tricks and they usually responded to my commands over anybody else's. Achilles and Hector both had big pleading eyes and were constantly playing, digging holes, sniffing around and mangling toys in our fenced-in yard.

They were total adrenaline addicts; you know how beagles are.

The teachers at school told Mom that Palmer had attention deficit disorder, but he always got an A in every class he took. He got picked on a lot in school but never seemed to mind, even while I was storming around in a rage about it; he'd watch me pacing with a slight smile on his face. As the years went by, he only became more withdrawn. I too had my own contradictions, such as the fact that I pitied and envied him at the same time. My friends, their little brothers were pains in the ass, always finding what their older brothers did more exciting and worldly and therefore pestering them. Palmer never pestered me. In fact, I tried to get his attention and approval more often than he did mine. After a while I stopped, and we both simply assumed that there would be days when Palmer would wander into traffic and I would be there to pull him back before he got run over.

During one hot summer, Dad built a doghouse for the beagles and put out a small kiddie pool for them. As puppies, we had let them live in the house but Mom put her foot down about the unrelenting mess they made, calling them her two other kids. The beagles had thoroughly destroyed the yard; Mom wanted to save the house.

I took a double-armful of scrap wood, a paper bag full of nails, a hammer and an old blanket and marched into the trees, Palmer in tow, rubbing his hands like a mad scientist and saying moo-hoo-ha-ha. First, I let him pick a tree; on his second try he picked one that looked good to me, one that would support a clubhouse. I built part of the structure on the ground, then hammered in the steps, climbed up and had him help me lift it up and set it between the strongest branches. After about two hours, I had created a monstrous-looking, but functional, treehouse, complete with the old blanket I had nailed up as a door.

"It's not that big," I told him. "But it could fit maybe you and a friend of yours."

"It's perfect," Palmer said, his eyes gleaming.

"So now you have a clubhouse. Who're you going to invite into your club?"

"Nobody," said Palmer. "I have no friends."

"I'll join your club," I said, feeling sorry for him. "And since the club was your idea you can be the president."

"No," Palmer told me. "You can't join. Nobody can join. It's my secret."

And with that, he climbed up and inspected the treehouse.

He shouted down at me from his fortress: "Will this roof leak?"

"Maybe Dad will give me some shingles to put on it."

"Yes, yes, let's do that. It can't get wet in here ever."

"All right," I said, still stung by his rejection.

"And anyway, it's not a clubhouse."

"What is it?"

"It's a church. My church. I'm going to worship God here."

He laughed, crawling inside the treehouse and disappearing from my view.

"You're fucking weird, Jesus," I told him.

He didn't answer—didn't even threaten to tell Mom I used the F word.

After a while, I gathered up the hammer and leftover nails and went home.

•

I wake up on Saturday morning determined, restless and craving work and routine, anything to keep my mind focused until enough time passes that I can forget ten years of marriage.

As a mental health professional, I know several methods of managing stress.

Tense an area of muscles on your body for a few seconds, then relax for ten to thirty seconds. Move to the next part of your body. Repeat.

Imagine that a part of your body feels heavy and warm. Focus on the feet, hands, shoulders, arms and legs. This is called autogenic training.

Employ breathing techniques to learn to control your breathing so that you take deep, infrequent breaths.

Use cognitive restructuring techniques to teach your brain to handle stress in specific ways.

Meditate. This can be used in conjunction with other techniques.

Imagine a special place that makes you feel at peace with the world, such as a sunny beach. Attain a feeling of calm and rest in this special secret place and hold it for five minutes.

Your body will also manage stress for you if you choose not to do it yourself:

Insomnia.

Irritability and mood swings.

Nervous ticks.

Loss of appetite.

Depression.

Clearly, I would have to take care of my feelings about Jenny leaving me—in other words, Jenny sleeping with another man—or else my body would. Between dealing with my wife's infidelity and my brother's insanity, I hardly slept at all the night before.

Late into the night, until I finally drifted off, I heard Palmer pacing around the house, fiddling with stuff. Probably installing his monitoring devices and alarms.

Now that I think of it, I have barely slept all week. When you don't sleep enough, patterns of electrical activity that happen in your brain during sleep are interrupted, which can mess up your ability to do even simple things.

It can also make you paranoid, and I don't need that right now. Last night, I was actually considering borrowing some of Palmer's gear, tracking down my wife, and spying on her. As if that would get her back. As if getting her back is exactly what I want or need.

I'm not sure what I want. Or need.

Okay, I love her and want her back and all, but if she did come back I'm not sure that this would be a good thing. She did cheat on me and leave me, and nothing we would say or do would ever change that. We'd go ahead with our plan to have kids and grow old together and retire in some sunny place like Phoenix, hoping that would solve our problems, but it wouldn't; it'd only make everything worse. No matter what we did, our marriage would forever be haunted by a ghost that would never go away and couldn't be ignored.

What I should really want is for her to be happy and to move on with my own life, but I'm not there yet.

The morning sun shines through the sheer white window curtains that Jenny had picked out and I had hung up. The sunlight is a pale gold, reminding you that it's cold outside, making you feel even more warm and safe inside. How I love the fall.

On a day like this, you can honestly feel like you can make things turn around. In the morning, you forget that your big bed feels empty without your wife lying next to you.

After a long shower, I have a cup of coffee, throw on a sweatshirt and go outside to do some yardwork. This is my all-time favorite non-hokey way of relieving stress: Get busy and start working. Work that doesn't require your brain to do anything. That's how the Buddhist monks have done it for centuries. They perform manual labor to blank out the mind. Ask yourself how many Buddhist monks are nuts. Not many, I would think.

Keith, a friend of mine, does it with computer games, going into a state of excitement-catatonia, as he calls it. Dobbs, he loves model trains and has a big HO set-up in his basement. Everybody's got their way of venting the pressure that builds up inside.

I go into the shed, pull down a rake and use it to start gathering up the leaves that now carpet the yard. Big brown oak leaves. I like the sound the leaves make, *chih chih chih*. To me, the sound of leaves being raked is the sound of good clean honest work.

My conscious mind blanks out after a while, but my subconscious keeps trying to work out my problems the whole time. That's how I solve a lot of my problems; I tuck them away into my subconscious. Days later, the solution will come to me in the shower or while I'm driving my truck home from work.

My problem is this:

I work as a psychiatric orderly making about twelve dollars an hour helping patients under the supervision of nurses and doctors. Up in New York City, you can make fourteen or even fifteen dollars. I found this occupation when I was in the Air Force.

After I was discharged, I married Jenny and had to support us. I did some research and found out that there was going to be a twenty-five percent increase in the amount of jobs available among psychiatric aides over the next ten years. There was an endless supply of nuts. A real growth industry. People were getting nuttier by the minute.

Now I don't have the wife, don't need the job, don't even need this house in the middle of a nice quiet little town.

Basically, I can do anything I want.

And there it is. This is my problem.

It's a good problem to have, I know. Even though it scares the hell out of me. For the first time ever, I have real choices of what to do with my life.

It's weird, but when you're comfortable, you long for change, but when things change on you, all you can think about is getting your comfort back.

My brother comes out of the house, stretching and yawning, and without a word starts helping me with the yardwork. For a while, we work side by side in silence. I don't mind his presence, as long as he behaves himself. It's a nice fall day, sunny and crisp. Being outside in the clean cool air fills me with energy, makes me want to play football.

After an hour, I pause, lean on my rake and say, "I think I'm going back to school."

Palmer looks at me and I look at him. He is skinnier than I remember him being back in high school. Wearing black and with his long dirty-blond hair pulled back into a ponytail, he looks like some washed-up German rocker. Seeing us, you'd hardly know we're brothers.

"Chad, can I tell you something?"

Uh-oh, I think, hearing his tone. Here it comes.

He says, "It's important. It might affect what kind of decisions you're going to be making about your life."

Imagine a special place that makes you feel at peace with the world.

A sunny beach. Anyplace warm and safe.

Attain a feeling of calm and rest.

Hold it for five minutes.

"Go ahead," I tell him. At this point, I just want the suspense over with and actually want him to spill his insanity on me. "I'm ready."

He says, "It's okay. I debugged the yard as well as the house last night. I did another sweep this morning. We're clean. Plus I've got our own monitoring devices all around."

"Good."

I'm picturing myself walking around my own house wondering if I'm being watched, not by the bad guys, but by Palmer.

He says, "I've also got eighty thousand dollars in cash upstairs. If you want to quit your job, quit your job. We don't have to work at all for a while. We'll have some time to think. You can go to school. But first I need you to do something for me."

I blink at him. "What do you want, Palmer?"

He says, "I want you to forget everything you know. I want you to open your mind."

Palmer is going to drag me down with him, just when I'm starting to think about piecing myself back together.

Just when I think I have a real choice.

To be honest, though, I'm kind of relieved. Strange as it sounds, going on Palmer's loony ride feels like comfort to me, like home. We're playing our old roles again, performing our mutual therapy.

Palmer is lost and needs care.

I'm lost and need somebody to take care of.

Maybe helping him will be good for me. Maybe, if I try to heal him, I can heal myself.

And maybe, just maybe, I can get to have the brother I always loved but never knew.

# 6

Palmer puts down his rake and asks me to take a walk with him to see the old treehouse. This is symbolic, I know; he is telling me that he is letting me inside. He's finally going to let me in the club. Me, I simply can't resist the offer to get inside his head for the first time in my life. I have to see. I'm game for the hike.

We cross the street, pass the ballfield, and tramp deep into the woods.

Even fifteen years later, Palmer knows where to go. He spent a lot of time out here. Our boots crunch leaves and the air has a bite to it. The trees look bare and honest. The air smells a little bit like smoke. The ground is carpeted with brown leaves and dead branches and twigs. It's a time and place to breathe deep, and I do so, enjoying the air and the season. The act of walking gives me a sense of putting things behind me.

In New York, Palmer says, there are always tons of people walking around at all times day and night. It's a large, crowded city, and everything is at your fingertips.

In the country, he tells me, you don't see anybody and at night the town is dead. You can't call up a deli and order a sandwich and coffee. You have to get in your car and drive five miles to find a 7-11 and get a pack of cigarettes.

He shudders.

"I hate the country," he says. "I feel trapped. It's scary. I actually feel safer in New York."

"It's home to me," I tell him. "And there's no place safer."

"Somebody could kill right you right on the street in New York, but people will see it. I don't mind the idea of dying alone, but I don't want to die unobserved."

"Uh-huh," I tell him.

"Hey, there's the treehouse. I see it."

Together we approach the big tree, summoning up our own private memories of the past, mine dealing with rejection, Palmer's probably dealing with belonging.

"What did you do out here all the time, Palmer?"

The treehouse looks old and worn and filled with the debris. The old blanket is gone. But the treehouse is still useful, I can see. It still looks sturdy enough. Other kids can use it if they find it. I pull my hands out of my pockets and test one of the boards held into the tree by two rusty nails, used as a step in the ladder up to the treehouse. It still holds.

"This is where it all started," he says quietly.

"What started?"

I turn to face Palmer, but instead of answering my question, he tells me that the U.S. government performed radiation experiments on people and kept it a secret for decades.

The government also knew that atom bomb testing in Nevada and Utah in the '50s was giving its own citizens cancer and kept that secret, too.

Tobacco companies still won't tell you what's in their cigarettes or admit that nicotine is addictive. The FDA still doesn't regulate cigarettes.

The CIA knocked off foreign leaders, conducted LSD research on unwitting Americans, recruited journalists to help them in foreign intelligence operations, and planted stories in the foreign press, hoping they would be picked up in the domestic press.

The Army conducted drug research on its own soldiers and sprayed San Francisco, the Pentagon and the New York City subway system with germs as part of its biological warfare testing program.

The FBI infiltrated and illegally harassed radical organizations in the '60s; at one time, it even developed its own chapter of the KKK.

Richard Nixon's "plumbers" conducted illegal espionage against the Democratic Party, resulting in the Watergate scandal.

Among the Watergate burglars were Cuban exiles who had been involved in the CIA campaign to assassinate Fidel Castro. A conspiracy theorist was the first to point that out.

Palmer tells me that film director Oliver Stone once said, "Paranoids have all the facts."

The Roman historian Tacitus once said, "Rumor is not always wrong"—stuff like the Iran-Contra arms for hostages deal and other things that leaders "can't recall."

The German philosopher Nietzsche once said, "Joyous mistrust is a sign of health."

Palmer wants to know what I think about all of that.

I told Palmer that I'd keep an open mind, so I decide to go with the flow.

"Well, I heard about Watergate and that the tobacco companies have politicians in their back pocket, and the rest are good conspiracy theories, I guess."

"They're not theories, Chad. They really happened."

"I know you believe they happened—"

"No, I'm not saying they happened as in I believe they happened. They really did happen. I'm not kidding. If you don't believe me, ask the government."

"All right," I say warily. "Fine. They happened."

"There is a definite difference between conspiracy history and conspiracy theory. Now, if you know that these things happened, you have to realize a few things. First of all, the government can keep secrets. In fact, it kept stuff like radiation experiments and drug and germ warfare experiments on U.S. citizens a secret for decades until the Freedom of Information Act came along and let us peek behind the curtain. You should also realize that most of these events, which are now known as history, started as conspiracy theories. Watergate, for example, was just a theory until *The Washington Post* cracked the story."

"It was bound to happen," I say. "The government is too dumb to keep secrets."

"It happens. The government keeps tons of secrets."

"It's not one big cohesive entity," I explain to him. "It's a giant organization made up hundreds of departments and sections—"

"A single moment of time is made up of many billions of events," Palmer says. "The government has secrets and spends about three billion dollars a year protecting them. That's a lot of secrets. So if we know that these horrible things happened years ago, what else could have that we don't know about? And what could be happening right now?"

"Well, that's the problem with conspiracy theorists," I say. "They see little bunches of facts, see smoking guns, and then make connections. I guess it depends on a lot of things. Like if you trust the government. A lot of people don't trust the government these days. It also depends on your imagination, or whether you accept that shit happens. Some people can't take coincidences or just plain chance, so they say there must be a conspiracy."

"Or you could say that if you see suspicious coincidences, make connections and believe that a crime was plotted and executed by a group of individuals, then you have your very own conspiracy theory."

I shrug. "Fine. That's a nicer way of putting it."

"It should be nice. Theories are a first step to getting at the truth. Sure there are a lot of bad ones. But that's true of science, too. Remember that the idea that the world is round was just a theory promoted by a small group of men considered insane in their time."

"If you're going to compare today's conspiracy theorists to them, then you are crazy."

"You've already decided that I'm not crazy."

"No," I say, "you're wrong about that. The truth is I haven't made up my mind yet. Sure, you're talking real reasonable, but you have to pass the test."

Palmer squints at me, but he's smiling, he's amused. "What's the test?"

"I want to see if over the next few days you can talk about anything except conspiracies," I say. "And I haven't heard yet how you're somehow at the center of the biggest conspiracy of all, so big that you need spy gadgets to protect yourself."

"Fair point," Palmer says, still smiling. "We'll get to mine later."

"No conspiracy you tell me would surprise me, Palmer," I say. I'm trying to be completely rational, hoping this will keep him rational. He had opened the door to let me inside, but I still feel like I'm outside. I need to keep him talking.

I say, "I've heard them all."

The international banking conspiracy. The Zionist conspiracy. The media conspiracy. The Vatican conspiracy. The international communist conspiracy. The Aquarian conspiracy—

Palmer says, "You didn't hear about the biological warfare experiments the Army conducted, in which they sprayed the population of San Francisco with germs."

"I had heard that one. But I thought it was a conspiracy theory."

Immediately, I flinch. Palmer caught me in a trap.

One world government. The New World Order. The United Nations. The Council on Foreign Relations. The World Bank. The International Monetary Fund. The World Health Organization. Bilderbergers. Rothschilds. Rockefellers. The Trilateral Commission—

"Listen," I tell him. "The problem with all this is that there are too many conspiracy theories. There's a conspiracy theory for everything. Princess Diana dies in a car crash or JFK Jr. goes down in his plane that he wasn't qualified to fly at night, and everybody screams conspiracy. Every major thing in the news becomes a conspiracy. It's noise, Palmer. If too many conspiracy theories come out, we won't take them seriously anymore. We'll miss the real conspiracies. People will block them out. They don't want to hear it. It makes them anxious and want to hide. It makes the media laugh instead of look. So much noise fills up and you've got a perfect smokescreen for the real bastards to do what they want, and if somebody makes a theory about the real shit that's going down, it'll be just more noise. There's never any closure."

Palmer says nothing. He seems to be considering my ideas, chewing on them. He holds out his hand and runs it along the bark of his favorite tree. Somewhere far off we can hear a chainsaw going, carving firewood.

FBI CIA NASA FEMA GWEN HAARP CDC ATF WHO WTO DEA—

"Sure, real conspiracies happen," I tell him. "It gets absurd, though, when you hear about a vast conspiracy orchestrating all major world events, especially when they get so big they tie the JFK assassination to Pearl Harbor to the Trilateral Commission to George Bush and every other president we've had. The conspiracy gets so big that everything that ever happened is part of it. It gets so big that history itself is a conspiracy theory. That's crazy."

"Absurdity doesn't mean falsehood," Palmer says. "Tertullian, an early father of the Catholic Church, said, '*Et sepulus resurrexit; certum est quia impossibile est,*' which basically means, 'The resurrection of Christ is therefore credible, just because it is absurd.'"

Fascism. Human Genome Project. Multinational corporations. MI6. Division-5. The Mossad. Illegal taxation. Totalitarianism. Alien cover-ups. Faked landings on the Moon. Giant faces carved into the surface of Mars. JFK. The Program. The Dark Alliance. Freemasons. The Insiders. The Federal Reserve. House of Morgan. The Mafia—

He adds, "'Doubt is not a pleasant condition, but certainty is absurd.' Voltaire."

"Fine," I say. "Again, it's a nice way of putting it. But most conspiracy theorists are either trying to make a buck or they're outright nuts. You have to admit that. Believe me, I deal with paranoid schizophrenics all the time at the hospital. They're always telling me they have expensive electronic gear in their heads, their eyeballs or the ass. They're always telling me that a secret U.N. army is hiding in Mexico, its generals flying around in black helicopters, and they're going to invade America. And I ask them, okay, well, when are they going to get around to it? If these secret societies have been taking over the world for a thousand years or whatever, when the hell are they going to finally get around to doing it? This is what I mean about there being no closure. The conspiracy never ends; it just gets bigger. Me, I actually want to get on with my life. I also want to have a few idealistic thoughts about my country. You want to tell me that the government and Big Business screws the little guy, I say fine, tell me something I don't know. But in the meantime, I want to be happy without somebody telling me vast evil forces are taking over."

"Ignorance is bliss, then," he says bitterly. "You're happy with your head in the sand."

"It's too much information, Palmer. It destroys people's innocence, makes them less happy, more anxious about living their life, which already has plenty of challenges. For example, in case it hasn't really sunk into you due to your own problems, my wife just left me. Hearing too much of this conspiracy crap infects you like a sickness, makes you skeptical of everything that you read and hear and see. It makes you want to question everything."

Palmer smiles. He tells me to cheer up.

"You're becoming a better American already," he says.

Maybe he's right about that, I tell myself. But if that's true, then I was right all along about one thing. All good Americans are nuts.

Years ago, you were a nut if you didn't completely trust the government; today, you're a nut if you do. Figure that one out.

Chemtrails in the skies. Fluoride in the water. Low-frequency EMF in the air. Mercury fillings in your teeth. Subliminal messages on TV. Elvis. Bill Gates. George Bush. John Tesh. Nazis. Cabalists. Rosicrucians. Hermetic Order of the Golden Dawn. Priory of Sion. Royal Society. Nimrod. Knights of Malta. Golden Triangle. Mena. Black helicopters—

He says, "Conspiracies happen all the time. Forget the rhetoric of evil invisible empires pulling the puppet strings. Just admit that if you operate in an environment of secrecy, then you will have certain temptations. Two CIA guys are talking and one says if only so-and-so would disappear, then we would have better relations with China. They keep talking about it and then one day, guess what, the guy disappears. Now two rich guys in Big Business, dripping with millions, dirty with it, they golf together and go to the same parties and their kids are going to Yale together, one says to the other, if only my factory did a little better in this safety inspection, we could do more business together and make many more millions. Later on, the inspection is altered and everybody's happy except for the workers who keep getting mutilated in accidents. The CIA is not evil and neither are the FBI or Big Business; these organizations are just what they say they are. But certain people operating inside these environments of secrecy can't help but take some shortcuts here and there if they think it's for a good cause, and after enough shortcuts, it becomes a regular thing, maybe gets bigger and more ambitious. So you can see that you don't need a vast organization to change the course of the country, such as putting the economy into a recession or knocking off a president or starting a war. Money is power. So is information. Just look at the fact that a kid on the Internet can change the price of a company's stock through disinformation. Consider that a rogue trader can bring down one of England's oldest banks through disinformation. Consider somebody like that guy, John Douglass, who runs the Fed. Look at what happens when he says the Fed is raising interest rates. Some guy who has nothing to do with you or the company you work for, well, he has this meeting and then you lose your job."

Area 51. Concentration camps. Underground bases. Germ warfare. Cattle mutilations. Assassinations. Information. Disinformation. Teletubbies.

"Fine," I say. "So where are you taking me with all this?"

"I just want you to understand and believe that a small group of men who have a common purpose, patience, money and the ability to operate in secrecy can control the world."

It's cold out and getting colder.

I shake my head wearily and start back for the house, Palmer tagging along like a puppy, going on about various plots and villains and speculations, probing me, trying to find where I personally draw the line between sanity and insanity, possible and impossible.

He says, "'If you would be a real seeker after truth, it is necessary that at least once in your life you doubt, as far as possible, all things.' Rene Descartes."

"Right," I say.

He says, "'Man's most valuable trait is a judicious sense of what not to believe.' Euripides."

"Fine," I say.

Me, all I wanted to know was what Palmer did out here, up in his treehouse, all those years.

•

The International Banking Conspiracy: Some conspiracy theorists believe that the Federal Reserve is a mechanism to create dependence on a small group of powerful international bankers, who can manipulate the money supply to create booms and busts. Others believe that it is a mechanism to enslave the United States to foreign creditors.

The controversy over a national bank started soon after the Constitution was signed. Some of the Founding Fathers believed that it would result in debt and inflation and dependence on a rich aristocracy. Thomas Jefferson wrote, "I sincerely believe . . . that banking establishments are more dangerous than standing armies."

The First Bank of the United States was nonetheless incorporated but Congress did not renew its charter after twenty years because it caused inflation.

The Second Bank of the United States was chartered because the War of 1812 resulted in mammoth costs. This event forever linked international banking conspiracy theories to the concept that war results in national debt and subsequent deep dependence on private banking interests. From then on, most wars would be blamed on international bankers.

Andrew Jackson, the populist War of 1812 hero who became president in 1832, called the national bank a "curse to the republic; inasmuch as it is calculated to raise around the administration a moneyed aristocracy dangerous to the liberties of this country." He said to the bankers of his day, "You are a den of vipers and thieves. I intend to rout you out, and by the Eternal God, I will rout you out." Jackson vetoed the bill to renew the bank's charter and then survived the first assassination attempt of an American president by a "lone gunman." By the end of his second term as president, Old Hickory had wiped out the national debt.

During the great panics in 1873, 1893 and 1907, scared depositors made a run on one bank, which sparked runs on others, exhausting deposits. Many lost their savings. In the Great Panic of 1907, a rumor circulated that a bank had failed, sparking the run. Some conspiracy theorists believe that J.P. Morgan, the robber baron who made millions in steel, railroads and banking, started these rumors to ultimately benefit himself.

Said Woodrow Wilson of the Great Panic of 1907, who would later become president, "All this trouble could be averted if we appointed a committee of six or seven public-spirited men like J.P. Morgan to handle the affairs of our country."

In 1910, J.P. Morgan held a private meeting with six other powerful international bankers on Jeckyll Island. The robber barons of the day were well accustomed to buying lawmakers and judges, manipulating the stock market and being vicious in business. It is alleged by conspiracy theorists that these men conceptualized a new national bank at this meeting. This time, the bankers did not call their idea a central or national bank.

Instead, they called it the Federal Reserve System.

Once their man Woodrow Wilson was elected president, the bill could be passed. Even then it took some time to market the idea to the public. In 1913, during Wilson's second term, the Federal Reserve Act was passed by Congress and signed into law by Wilson.

Today, the Fed is made up of twelve Federal Reserve banks, each dedicated to a section of the country. They are overseen by a board of governors appointed by the president. However, the system is not a federal institution. It is a private organization. The member banks own it and these, in turn, are owned by their major stockholders.

Wall Street watches everything that the chairman of the board of governors says and does. Significant changes in the interest rate can create inflation, upset markets, wreck or enrich companies, destroy jobs, and make or lose fortunes.

Inflation reflects the imaginary worth of a dollar after you increase or decrease the supply of money, which is controlled by private interests. If the dollar goes down in value due to high inflation, prices are adjusted to inflation and your dollar suddenly buys less.

Said Congressman Charles A. Lindbergh, Sr. in 1913, "This Act establishes the most gigantic trust on earth. . . . When the President signs this act, the invisible government by the money power, proven to exist by the Money Trust Investigation, will be legitimized. This new law will create inflation whenever the trusts want inflation."

What he meant was that a small group of hugely rich men could swing inflation and rack up incredible profits as a result.

The Fed banks are privately owned banks, but if one of them goes out of business, U.S. taxpayers must foot the bill.

Banks charge interest on their loans to make money. To banks, debt is profit.

As debt goes up, so does the cost of interest to the government. This cost must be paid each year. Each year, every dollar that is paid to the banks and foreign creditors cannot be spent by the government on the military, social programs or anything else- unless the government is willing to go even deeper into debt.

Of course, the government itself is the real blame. Politicians overspend. You know, pork barrel legislation tacked on pet projects for home states. The Democrats overspending on social programs. The Republicans overspending on the military and missile defense and handing away trillions in tax cuts.

Conspiracy theorists say this does not matter. The mechanism of the Federal Reserve, they say, allows foreign nations and international banking interests to own most of the U.S. national debt—creating dependence on those foreign nations and bankers.

Henry Ford, the father of Ford Motor Company, once said, "It is well enough that the people of the nation do not understand our banking and monetary system for, if they did, I believe there would be a revolution before tomorrow morning."

Said the late U.S. Senator Barry Goldwater, "International bankers make money by extending credit to governments. The greater the debt of the political state, the larger the interest returned to the lenders." The same goes for people. Americans continue to go into debt faster than their incomes can increase.

Goldwater said, "We recognize that the Rothschilds and Warburgs of Europe and the houses of J.P. Morgan, Kuhn, Loeb and Company, Schiff, Lehman and Rockefeller possess and control vast wealth." He added, "How they acquire this vast financial power and employ it is a mystery to us." When he talked about the "Rothschilds and Warburgs of Europe," he was referring to the ancient and powerful European banking dynasties.

Said James Warburg, testifying before the U.S. Senate Foreign Relations Committee in 1950, "We shall have world government whether you like it or not—by conquest or consent."

# 7

Today is Monday and first thing I pick up the phone and call out sick again. Then I go out to the supermarket to run some errands and pick up groceries. While I'm out, Lee Charles Jackson, the President of the United States, is assassinated at 11:37 a.m. Eastern Standard Time.

I find this out when I come home and the first thing I see is my brother sitting on the recliner, watching the instant replay of the shooting on TV.

"Hey, Chad," he says, without looking at me.

"Hey, Palmer," I say mechanically, kicking off my shoes. "It's pretty cold out there today. So what are you watching?"

"CNN. The President just got shot."

Holding the grocery bags in my arms, I watch the TV in a stunned silence.

President Jackson steps out of some building, waving and smiling, surrounded by reporters, Secret Service men in their dark sunglasses, and well wishers.

Jackson is a popular, activist president who knows how to get things done without spending a lot of money. I had voted for him, even though he is a Democrat.

Jackson had two pet programs that did require a lot of money, however. He had wanted us to go to Mars and had doubled NASA's spending starting in his last term. A lot of people had been skeptical about this, but the new technologies that came out of the boom in research had resulted in new consumer industries, which in turn had created a bonanza for the economy. The Mission to Mars project had been more than an act of will and imagination; it was economic policy. Jackson called it the only good part of supply side economics: If you increase technology, you get economic growth without much inflation.

Meanwhile, the space industry had developed to the point that companies were actually starting to lease shuttle time to send rich tourists into space or to the Moon.

Buying stock in one of those companies was one of the smartest things I have ever done—not enough stock to make me rich, granted, but it's there.

Now, halfway through his second term, Jackson started telling America about his second program. He was going to set up a special fund for the budget surplus and pay off the national debt within ten years. That, and the Mission to Mars, were going to be his legacy.

The camera does a crazy tilt and I get a sense that everybody is shouting and running around. I hear these strange flat popping sounds, which is how gunshots sound on video. President Jackson falters, his arm still high in the air in mid-wave, his face wearing this weird, puzzled look, and then he is lost in a sea of white men.

Somebody had fired five shots from a pistol into the President's chest and stomach.

What Jackson was thinking right then, I would give anything to know.

I mean, here you are the most powerful man in the world, surrounded by these fanatical Secret Service guys and all the best protection money can buy, and somebody can walk up to you and gun you down in broad daylight.

I would look surprised, too, if that happened to me.

Actually, though, when you consider it's that easy, and when you consider all the nuts in the world, especially in the United

States, it doesn't make you wonder how these things can happen. It makes you wonder how they don't happen more often.

A nut sprays the White House with machine-gun fire and you shake your head and go, oh that figures.

The Unabomber mails pipe bombs to Federal judges and you don't get appalled. Instead, you think, boy am I glad I'm not a Federal judge.

My brother reaches into a big bowl of popcorn, grabs a handful, and shoves it into his mouth.

The assailant is restrained in about another two seconds. Four guys in suits had jumped on him in a kind of cop ballet. First his arms were clamped. One suit grabbed his neck and forced his head down while the gun was taken away from him. Then they did a sweep that landed the assassin face first onto the sidewalk, where he was cuffed.

Palmer says he knows those maneuvers that cops use and can teach them to me if I want. With the right training, he says, your reflexes can respond like lightning.

Meanwhile, all these other guys in suits come out of the woodwork holding Uzis and pistols, scanning the area, forming a human wall around the President. Jackson is whisked into his limo, which takes off with a screech before the door is even closed.

Lying on the ground are two men, who turn out later to be the Secretary of State and an Illinois Congressman. I feel sorry for those guys, left behind on the sidewalk in pools of their own blood, their legs twitching.

End of footage. History had been made in several seconds.

The news anchor comes on and in a grave voice tells America that the President is in critical condition at an undisclosed hospital.

Holding the grocery bags, I feel several things all at once.

Awe that this kind of thing could happen.

Panic that my President might die.

Rage that somebody would shoot the President of the United States.

A desire to blame and hold somebody accountable for it.

Frustration that I couldn't see more because of the crazy camera tilt.

I'm American, and something big has just happened to America. For a moment, I forget all about my sorry life and get caught up in this thing that has engulfed all of us. I stand there in a state of shock that only comes when real drama happens right in front of you.

Another cheap thrill.

Overall, I suppose, what I feel is this huge sense of vulnerability.

Palmer is wolfing down popcorn out of the bowl, which is now half-empty. At his feet, kernels litter the carpet that Jenny had picked out to "go with the room."

"They're going to show it again," he says.

I sit on the couch, still holding the bags, my eyes glued to the television.

"Those people you were talking about, they did this?"

Palmer turns to me and winks. "Of course not. It was a crazed lone gunman."

Then he laughs derisively.

I say, "You're a sick fucker, Palmer." As if it is all his fault.

The thing is, to me, it kind of is.

Palmer merely shrugs.

The other thing I'm thinking is, if this is all real, then they really are out to get my brother, and I don't want him anywhere near me.

Assassinations happen, and most people don't want to hear the truth. They want to be fed the company line, know that justice has been served, and move on with their lives.

"I'll bet they find a copy of *Catcher in the Rye* in the guy's house or in his jacket," Palmer is saying. "After conditioning, you need to give the subject a token or catch phrase that will pull the trigger and set your little robot into motion. After Mark David Chapman shot John Lennon in the back, he sat down and started reading *Catcher in the Rye*. John Hinkley, Jr. also had it. It's an inside joke, get it? J.D. Salinger was in the Army Counterintelligence Corps. Same unit as Henry Kissinger, I believe. Go figure."

Palmer is definitely going to drag me down with him. I can feel myself opening up to him. I'm completely vulnerable. Every nutty thing he says now has credibility. In fact, the nuttier it sounds, the more credibility it suddenly has with me.

"They always have three names, those assassins," Palmer says. "John Wilkes Booth. Mark David Chapman. Lee Harvey Oswald. Crazed lone gunman."

He says, "This one isn't a Roman Catholic. That'll come out. I guarantee it. If you look at history, though, many assassins are. Roman Catholics killed Garfield and McKinley, but botched on Teddy Roosevelt, FDR and Harry Truman. Woodrow Wilson's nurse, a Catholic, finished him off. That's the work of the Church, not us. The Catholic Church is the ancient enemy of the Illuminati. They've been fighting their war, behind the scenes, for two thousand years."

"The Catholic Church is involved in assassination?"

"Not the Church itself, but an element of it formed secretly to fight the Illuminati centuries ago. Not even the Pope knows about its existence today. But the Black Popes do."

I haven't slept in days. Palmer predicted that Jackson would be shot, and I just watched it happen on television. Both combine now to completely freak me out.

"Dick Croshaw, the Vice President, is already in Washington, ready to be sworn in," he tells me. "He's their guy. Their guy's in charge now. And we won't be paying off any national debt any-time soon, believe me."

He reaches out and hands me a beer. I set down the bags and gratefully accept.

"So what happens now?" I ask feebly.

"Now," says Palmer, "in six days there will be a complete blackout across the entire eastern seaboard of the United States for twelve hours."

"No kidding," I say.

Imagine a special place that makes you feel at peace with the world.

He says, "Electricity is civilization."

Anyplace sunny and warm.

Palmer says, "It will be chaos and in that chaos, a hundred thousand people will die."

Hold it for five minutes.

# Part Two

# 8

The President has been shot and suddenly all the rules have changed.

The funny thing about all this conspiracy stuff is—now that it has credibility—the more I know about it, the less I believe what I have been told my whole life, and yet the more I admit that anything is possible. It's a real mindfuck, as they say in the Air Force.

Right now I'm feeling several emotions at once.

Irritated that Palmer might say, I told you so.

Irritated that he hasn't.

A strange sort of relief. I can almost hear a great big told-you-so coming from the collective consciousness of the country. Hearing what Palmer has said about the secret history of the world makes sense in this gut-paranoid kind of way.

Everybody has suspected at one time or another that the government, and the very world itself, is run by unseen powers, that everything else is a sham covering up this subtle brutality; this suspicion makes sense because life is that way. The average guy is always getting subtly, brutally screwed. It simply has to be some secret powers doing it.

When you're angry, you want an unjust world to make sense.

When you're angry, you need a scapegoat.

At the same time as feeling these things, I get this wave of panic. I wish Palmer never showed up. I like my little rabbit hole where I feel comfortable chasing a better lifestyle through consumption or whatever. Where I feel safe knowing that the government takes care of business. Where I know that there is a nonprofit out there fighting for every good cause so that I don't have to worry about them. I don't want to know the Truth. Maybe the bad guys have fed me a life of illusions, but they are illusions designed to keep me docile. They are good illusions. I want to be comfortable. If I didn't, I might have left Jenny first.

Before today, I would have told Palmer, "Those Masters of the World or whoever they are doing a good job. I like living here."

Then you hear that they assassinate a good president, put their man in charge of the most powerful nation on the earth, and are planning to promote further chaos, I am guessing, to create further dependence on government.

Hitler did that by having his men set fire to the Reichstag. He blamed it on the Communists and got President Hindenburg to go in with him and declare a national emergency, which by law allowed him to destroy the Weimar Republic and become a dictator with absolute power. Before that, Crassus seized power in Rome by forcing the slave general Spartacus to march on Rome instead of escape Italy; the panic-stricken Senate declared Crassus Praetor, which eventually led to the first triumvirate of Crassus, Pompeii and Julius Caesar and the rule of the emperors. Cicero, an enemy of Caesar, said that a vast right-wing conspiracy was bent on destroying the government, and hired men to terrorize Rome to prove it, hoping that Rome would put Cicero himself in power. The Gulf of Tonkin incident buried America in Vietnam. The sinking of the *Maine* got us into a war with Spain. The weird Zimmerman telegram and the sinking of the *Lusitania* got us into World War I. And speaking of conspiracy theories, there is a lot of evidence that Franklin D. Roosevelt pressured the Japanese into attacking Pearl Harbor so that he would have the excuse to declare war on Germany and pull America out of the Great Depression.

Devious minds throughout history have always known that humans will readily trade liberty for security. We Americans, for all our bluster, are no exception to this rule.

I don't have tons of schooling, I admit, but I do read a lot of books. I like history.

As Machiavelli said, "The end justifies the means."

I look over at Palmer and think about the old movie line, "He knows too much."

I think, Palmer lives in my house.

Immense plots and carefully laid plans, involving nations and presidents, have been set into motion centuries ago for some secret purpose that involve world domination, but all I want to know at this point if they are going to come and kill me.

•

The Illuminati Conspiracy: The historical Illuminati, whose actual name was the Order of Perfectibilists, was a secret society of secular humanists formed in Bavaria, Germany on May 1, 1776 by Adam Weishaupt, a university teacher and defrocked Jesuit. Weishaupt, who may or may not have been a real person (some believe that he was a secret committee of five people), founded the Illuminati for the "express purpose of rooting out all religious establishments, and overturning all the existing governments of Europe." He planned to create an egalitarian society under the dictatorship of the "illuminated," which would abolish private property, religion and feudalism—thinking that later influenced the propagation of a political philosophy called Communism. Once the masses became illuminated themselves, the dictatorship would wither away. The Illuminati was a pyramidal structure in which initiates advanced through a hierarchy of mysteries and learned ancient mystical secrets. Weishaupt believed in the time-tested principle of the end justifying the means; he said, "Our secret association works in a way that nothing can withstand, and man shall soon be free and happy." His code name was Spartacus. After Illuminati plans were discovered by the Bavarian authorities in the mid-1780s, the organization was outlawed by the government and banned by the Catholic Church. Conspiracy theorists believe that the organization did not disband entirely but went underground and spread Illuminati ideas to other countries, infiltrating the Priory of Sion and the Freemason lodges, already refuges for intellectuals and radicals, at their highest levels of leadership. Freemasonry, in turn, flowered until today it boasts more than five million members, the largest secret society in existence, despite the fact that the Catholic Church has called it a heretical religion. The organization traces its roots back to the medieval stonemasons who built the cathedrals, while others trace it even further to the architects of the pyramids and Solomon's Temple. The more esoteric aspects of its ideas can be traced to the Illuminati and Rosicrucians. Many groups are knockoffs of the Freemasons, such as the Knights of Columbus, Skull and Bones Society, Ku Klux Klan and others. John Wayne, Jesse Jackson, J. Edgar Hoover, Roy Rogers, Duke Ellington, Rudyard Kipling, Oscar Wilde, Earl Warren, Ronald Reagan, George Bush and many other Who's Who types were or are Freemasons, as were most of America's founding fathers. Freemasons were heavily involved in the French and American Revolutions and some conspiracy theorists say they engineered them. "Liberty, equality and fraternity" was practically a Freemason slogan. In the 1800s, after the ritual murder of the author of a book exposing their secrets, membership dropped dramatically for a while in the United States and some people even formed a new political party called the Anti-Masonic Party. Even back then—throughout history, actually, from ancient Rome to the present—people have been scared out of their wits by secret societies. Many conspiracy theorists consider the Illuminati and Freemasons to be essentially Satanist, as in certain texts Lucifer is admired as the bringer of light or secret knowledge. Conspiracy theorists also claim that the organization today continues to be a mechanism for the descendants of the Illuminati to continue their ancient plan to establish the New World Order. The more paranoid ones say the Illuminati itself is alive and well and behind everything.

Palmer tells me that he had worked for these people, the Illuminati.

"I was on the inside, Chad," he says. "Somebody gave me orders, and then I gave three different guys their orders, and so on, the way Amway would do a conspiracy. And the guy who gave me orders was one of the thirteen Masters of the World."

•

I say, "If you're who you say you are, tell me who killed JFK."

"A rogue element of the CIA," he says flatly. "We had absolutely nothing to do with that. Or Bobby, either. We don't run the world, Chad. We simply push its direction. Look at the media, for example. You can shape public opinion by owning the right piece of it. You don't have to buy up the entire industry. Then you can squash all the negative tobacco stories you want. The Catholic Church didn't do it either. After all, Kennedy was the first Catholic President."

I gape at him. I intended my request to be taken as sarcastic.

Seeing me stare at him, he adds, "All right. A lot of powerful people hated Kennedy's guts. They had motive and opportunity. But they wouldn't kill a President. Kennedy had threatened to dismantle the CIA, however. There were too many people making good money and entrenched in their own private foreign policy. Too many people would have been compromised, too many fortunes and careers flushed down the toilet. This rogue element of the CIA already owned a number of front companies, legal and illegal, and were pocketing the profits or using them to fund stuff nobody else in the government knew about. Kennedy was going to bring the whole house down, so some guys from CIA's Division-5 took him out. It had nothing to do with Castro. Dropped clues that the Cuban exile community was in on it, though. The Mafia also got heavily implicated, but only because of the discovered connections between them and the CIA. That's how Jimmy Hoffa got killed and thrown into a meat grinder, because he was about to expose those connections. Anyway, we're not the only conspiracy out there. There are tons of them. What most Americans don't know is that there were actually three planned attempts on Kennedy's life by right-wingers the year he was shot."

It sounds like the gospel truth. I feel like I'm sitting on this goldmine of information, knowing the answer to a question that has plagued thousands of Americans for decades. But who would believe me if I told them?

They'd say I'm a nut, of course.

Conspiracy theorists, even the ones who are right, are wackos in most people's book, including mine. Before today, that is.

Nobody wants to believe in secret societies, even though they're intrinsic to American society as a whole, from the Elks and Shriners to Freemasons and college fraternities.

People say those aren't secret societies, though—they call them societies with secrets.

The irony of all this makes me want to laugh.

Palmer says, "If the CIA hadn't done it, though, we probably would have. Kennedy had told the Treasury Department to print millions of dollars in U.S. notes, bypassing the Federal Reserve and taking a huge amount of money out of the international bankers' pockets."

"Stop," I say. "Start over. Tell me about how you came to work for them."

"They recruited me," he says, "when I was sixteen years old."

I stare at him, stunned.

"So that's why you left without leaving a note or anything."

Palmer sees the look I must have in my eyes right now.

"It had nothing to do with you, Chad."

I shake my head, feeling defensive. We're not ready to go there yet.

"Go back further," I said. "Who are these people, exactly?"

"I always kept tabs on you. When I left them, you were the only person I could turn to."

"Tell me who these people are, Palmer."

"I told you they call themselves the Illuminati," he says. "It means 'the illuminated.' It's an organization run by thirteen rich white men, the Masters of the World, who you never see in the media. The Masters belong to no organizations, even the suspicious ones like the Bilderbergers, the CFR and the Trilateral Commission. If I showed you a list of the fifty richest people in the world, you'd recognize names like the Rockefellers and Bill Gates, but you wouldn't recognize all fifty. These thirteen men you would never have heard of."

Vice President Croshaw is on the TV, giving a speech, saying something about the lone shooter being interrogated by the FBI.

I turn it off, irritated.

"They're already rich," I say. "What do they want, then?"

"They can never have enough money, because money gives them power, and that's what they really want. They want to set up a world government and change the world. They've been using the Freemasons and Rosicrucians and other groups for years to recruit their henchmen, and their top leadership, like me, they practically recruit from birth. I was born to be their man, so to speak. They watched me my entire life, and when I was ready, they recruited me. Don't ask me how." He snorts. "It involves astrology and ritualized magic."

"Are you saying these people killed Mom and Dad?"

I am out of my mind at this point.

"Relax, Chad," he says. "We're on the same side."

"Answer me or I'm getting my gun." I mean it.

"The honest answer is I don't know. I don't think so."

I glare at him, hating his honesty.

He says, "Listen to me. This is all important. The Illuminati is just a name, like any other secret society. For a while it actually existed in Germany in the 1700s until the Pope banned it and the Bavarian government outlawed it. The organization went underground, but that didn't matter. It was never the people who mattered in this fight, it was the ideas."

He stands and smiles down at me.

"Are you ready for the truth?" he says.

"I've heard the truth," I say, quoting *The X-Files*, "now I want the answers."

Palmer catches the reference and laughs.

I say, "You don't think they're going to kill you anymore, do you? You're too relaxed."

"I'm petrified," he says. "But after a while you realize if you're living on borrowed time, how great it is to be alive. I am loving life today. Because every day is my last day."

I swallow hard, nodding, and tell him to continue.

"You're going to hear a story," he says, "about an ancient war fought for the past two thousand years in Europe and the United States."

The scariest part of the rollercoaster ride is when you first get on and you're going up nice and slow, and you hear the *clack-clack-clack*.

He says, "As Jesus said, you will hear, but not comprehend. But when it all sinks in, it will blow your mind."

He asks me if I want to take a drive with him.

I ask him where he wants to go.

He tells me to take him to Mercer County Psychiatric Hospital, where I work.

# 9

While we're driving to the hospital, which is about a half-hour drive down to Trenton, Palmer tells me that the grand conspiracy of the Illuminati began two thousand years ago.

For two thousand years, he says, the Illuminati and the Catholic Church have viciously fought each other in a secret war. Even before the Church was officially founded in the fourth century, their schools of thought battled each other.

If you look at almost every conspiracy theory out there that sounds halfway normal, he goes on, it will tie into this grand conspiracy.

For two thousand years, many major historical events, mostly from the thirteenth century to the present, have been the result of Illuminati or Church influence or intervention.

As technology progressed and the world got steadily smaller, the war escalated.

This war is reaching its culmination now. And the Illuminati are winning.

Gripping the steering wheel, I'm barely listening to him. Instead, I'm sitting here wondering if my truck is bugged.

Seeing regular people on the streets of Riverdale, giving me little waves as I drive by, only makes me feel alienated. They are all asleep, I think. They have no idea of what's really going on, or that in six days the power will go out and this nice little town, like so many cities and towns, will go to hell.

It's like they don't exist anymore or something.

I recognize the symptoms and realize that suddenly I'm suffering from what's called a Cassandra Complex. Cassandra is this Trojan woman in mythology who was condemned by the gods to know the future but always be disbelieved when she tried to tell anybody what was going to happen. I'm sitting on a secret so big, so ridiculous, that nobody could believe me.

And a hundred thousand people will die.

I step on the gas pedal hard as we leave town and get onto Route 29.

"No so fast," Palmer says, eyeing me curiously. "One thing we definitely don't want is to attract the attention of a cop, even one of Riverdale's Finest. Do you understand?"

I nod, hunched over the wheel, grinding my teeth.

He says, "Always remember, these people play for keeps."

I feel like I've crossed some sort of line of belief. There is this concept I'm becoming familiar with called creeping bullshit. If you accept one idea as plausible and then start believing it, you can then find the next idea plausible and believe that one, too.

That's how some people hear stories about mutilated cows and wind up believing in UFOs, black helicopters, "men in black," and alien autopsies. It happens all the time.

If you buy into one article in a tabloid like *The Enquirer* or *The Weekly World News*, you might as well get a subscription.

Our grandmother's favorite article from one of the supermarket tabloids, which she kept on her refrigerator door in her last years before dying, was about rules of etiquette if Jesus showed up at your house for dinner.

She used to wear a plastic ball on a necklace that she had bought through an ad in one of those papers. In the ball was lucky dirt from Venus.

She loved that necklace. You couldn't talk her out of wearing it.

Like I keep saying, everybody has a propensity for being a nut at times. Think about it. Being nutty is a luxury of living in a rich country. You have more time on your hands, and your mind, no longer preoccupied with survival, is free to run amok.

It seems like I'm about to join the club.

"These people," Palmer tells me, "don't give warnings whose only effect is to force you to fight and defeat them. They don't make big speeches or send German models out of black helicopters to chase you like in the movie *Conspiracy Theory*. They don't blow everything up and riddle your apartment building with bullet holes, always one step behind you. You don't get taken prisoner so that you can be rescued later."

Nodding at Palmer, I tell myself that this is different. This is not creeping bullshit. I am not being suckered into a conspiracy theory and being turned into a nut. I was told the President was going to be shot, and he was. I was told that in six days the power will go out across the entire eastern United States, and I am ready to believe that it will happen, and that maybe I can do something about it.

The thing I'm wondering, though, is how much of what everything else Palmer tells me do I have to believe?

Palmer says, "They will kill you like the Mafia kills you, with a smile in front and a bullet in the brain from behind, nice and friendly and quiet. Or worse, somebody walks by you with an umbrella and pokes you, and you get a heart attack or a fast-acting cancer."

No, I tell myself. This is not Palmer suddenly telling me the earth is flat. What he has told me, despite any bullshit he might be laying on me, so far has shown itself to be all too real. I will let myself be skeptical about everything, but I do believe that President Jackson was assassinated by a group—not a lone gunman as the official story already being put out says—and that in six days the power will go out and people will die.

"Heart attack?" I say. "What do they inject you with?"

"Thiophosphate, a chemical found in insecticides. It gives you a sudden heart seizure, and you're dead. Even if anybody bothers to do an autopsy, they probably won't find it. That's how the Establishment got rid of J. Edgar Hoover, that queen who headed up the FBI for so many years, because he made too many enemies. They gave Jack Ruby, the guy who shot Lee Harvey Oswald right in the Dallas Police Station, a shot of cancer. In any case, killing you is all about expedience. Nobody cares about an assassination's dramatic value unless they want to hack you up to make an example out of you for others."

President Jackson died in the operating room just before we left the house. Vice President Croshaw was sworn in and is now America's new President.

Another coup d'etat in the world's most powerful democracy, while the rest of the country blinks and doesn't even notice.

"Basically," says Palmer, "if they want you dead, you're dead."

In six days, the power will go out. I am thinking that if there is nothing I can do—nothing anybody can do—to prevent it, then I really will go crazy.

•

The Media Conspiracy: This conspiracy alleges that the increasing concentration of ownership of the American mass media by a handful of multinational corporations is subverting the ability of the press to fulfill its role as the watchdog of democracy. Manipulating the media, however, is not new in American history. William Randolph Hearst and his "yellow press" helped stir up war fever that resulted in the Spanish-American War so that he could sell more newspapers. In 1977, Carl Bernstein, one of *The Washington Post* reporters who cracked the Watergate scandal, wrote an article for *Rolling Stone* that exposed the CIA's Operation Mockingbird, a twenty-five-year-long program in which more than four hundred journalists were recruited to help the CIA in foreign intelligence operations: "In many instances, CIA documents show," wrote Bernstein, "journalists were engaged to perform tasks for the CIA with the consent of the managements of America's leading news organizations." However, the scale and potential for manipulation today is a cause for concern among conspiracy theorists. In 1982, fifty corporations dominated the American mass media. By the year 2000, through merger, acquisition and deregulation, this number had fallen to ten: Time-Warner, Walt Disney Co., CBS, General Electric, Gannett, New York Times Co. and others. Meanwhile, news organizations are more focused on profit and dependent on advertising than ever, say media critics, resulting in commercialization of the news and a dumbing down of content, which is packaged to sell. What's more, it has become increasingly important to disseminate news faster and faster to stay competitive, resulting in an overreliance on corporate and government public relations at the expense of critical, unbiased investigative reporting. Some corporations have launched their own supposedly independent media watchdog organizations, whose real aim is actually to attack any of the media that challenges the corporate line, according to some media critics. The public, meanwhile, continues to depend on the media to tell it what news is important and, with the proliferation of pundits focusing news content on analysis instead of facts, what to think. A 1994 Veronis, Suhler & Associates study reported that the average American watches TV more than four hours per day, three hours listening to the radio and about a half-hour reading newspapers. According to Jacques Ellul, a French social historian, the guy who is most likely to be duped by propaganda is the "current events man," the guy who reads his newspapers and therefore sees himself as well-informed. According to Roger Ailes, chairman of Fox News (as told to *New York Magazine* in 1997), "People don't want to be informed; they only want the illusion of being informed." As a result, conspiracy theorists, activists and media critics allege, stories about corporate welfare, the acceleration of police surveillance capabilities, the trend towards monopolization of telecommunications, the transfer of nuclear secrets to China, and other stories were and are regularly censored. Meanwhile, top anchors and media executives rub elbows with Wall Street, government and business elites at secretive meetings of the Bilderbergers,

Trilateral Commission and Council on Foreign Relations; while top newsmen are invited to these meetings, they do not report on what they see and hear at them.

Conspiracy theorists want to know why.

•

"This is it," I tell Palmer, pulling into the parking lot. "Where I work."

Palmer looks at the plain, boxlike 1960s architecture and frowns. He wrinkles his nose, as if the place smells bad even from here.

"I can just picture it," he says. "Right out of *The Cuckoo's Nest*. I'll bet you actually expect people to get better in there."

I shrug and say, "Sometimes they do."

After I park the truck and shut off the ignition, I turn to Palmer and ask him what we're doing here. I am, after all, supposed to be sick and shouldn't be at work.

"We're going to see one of your patients," says Palmer. "Dr. Hiram Gaines, author of *Conspiracies Refound* and America's leading conspiracy theorist."

"He's one of the biggest nuts we got in there," I tell him.

Palmer winks as he gets out of the truck.

He pauses to tell me, "That's what you think."

# 10

Gaines does not look happy to see Palmer. The moment we enter the room, he takes an awkward step backward, then falls into his chair as if some unseen hand shoved him.

Palmer calmly takes off his jacket, smiling at him.

"Um, Dr. Gaines, I'd like you to meet my brother," I say.

Palmer holds up his hand for me to be quiet.

Gaines, sitting in his chair, won't take his eyes off of Palmer.

"Do I know you, sir?"

He looks scared as hell. He sniffs a little, as if Palmer has an aura that carries some old familiar smell that is both pleasant and repulsive.

"I know you," says Palmer. "The infamous author of *Conspiracies Refound*. Published two years ago by UpWord Publishing, Inc. of New York City, in hardcover, with a second printing in paperback earlier this year, six months before you walked in here and asked to be locked up. You're a genius at seeing the connections that reveal the secret plan of what you call the 'Invisible Empire.' You've become bit of a famous man, in a Fox Mulder kind of way, anyhow."

Gaines doesn't look like he's flattered. He is practically clawing at his beard, which he normally strokes deviously, a nervous tic. His face is pale. Even his lips are white.

"I should introduce myself," Palmer says, and steps forward to shake hands.

Gaines looks at Palmer's hand as if it's a snake.

"No offense, sir, but I would prefer not to shake hands with you." He glances at me. "You say he's your brother?"

I nod.

Palmer says, "I'll introduce myself differently, then. Ewige Blumenkraft."

Gaines' eyes bug out and he whispers, "Illuminati. I knew it."

This makes me jump. I have never heard Gaines use that word before in all of his paranoid rantings. His enemy was always the Invisible Empire.

"You took your time," he says to us. "I thought you would have killed me long ago."

Gaines looks like he's going to go ape. I tense, ready to restrain him if he lunges for Palmer's throat.

But nothing happens. Palmer is making a complex series of hand signals.

Visibly relieved, Gaines says over and over, "I understand."

He sighs and slouches in his chair.

"So you're fresh flown from the coop. Christ, I thought I was dead."

He goes on, "So you're lucky thirteen, it looks like. The Thirteenth Prince and the thirteenth Illuminatus to walk out of the light. You must be Palmer Carver. How hard it must be for you, Mr. Carver, on your first day out of the light."

Palmer smiles grimly. "They killed the President today."

Gaines nods. "Of course. He wanted to pay off the national debt." He glances at me smugly, as if to say I told you so.

"Next, they're going to shut off all the power on the eastern seaboard."

Gaines rubs his eyes and says, "I saw the connections, but I couldn't glue it together. I'm getting old and tired. So they're stepping up the schedule. I wonder how many Reichstag fires it will take. America is stubborn. Tell me about the blackout. How soon?"

"Six days."

"For how long?"

"Twelve hours."

"Christ on a bicycle."

I yell, "Wait a second. What the hell is going on here?"

Gaines ignores me and says, "Church countermeasures?"

Palmer ignores me and says, "I don't even know if they're aware it's going to happen. Their counterintel is probably reacting to Jackson getting killed. All the Christian Soldiers are most likely tied up looking into it. It's a great smokescreen, if you think about it. Kill the President so you can distract attention from the plan to shut off the power and cause chaos, accelerating the Plan."

"They are following the Law of Fives," says Gaines. "Jackson was three; the blackout makes four. What could the fifth event be, I wonder. I expect something big, really big, to happen after the power goes out. It'll make the blackout look like a children's ride at an amusement park."

He looks at the clippings on his walls longingly, as if he's itching to get back to researching connections and trying to predict the Illuminati's final move to complete the five.

Suddenly, his eyes wide with fear, he glances at me, then Palmer. "You don't think. . . ."

Palmer glances at me and says, "We shouldn't talk about that, Dr. Gaines. But to answer your question, yes, they might just do it. There is a reckless spirit in the organization these days. They might use Jehovah. They might go all the way and end the Game."

I'm trying to follow all of this helplessly.

Gaines takes off his glasses and rubs his eyes. "The sick, sick bastards."

Noticing my confusion, Palmer makes more hand signals at Gaines, who replies with his own, sometimes mixing phrases in Latin and German in a secret code.

*Via Crucis*, says Gaines.

*Via Lucis*, says Palmer.

Each exchange of phrases seems to unlock a door to a new phase in the conversation that takes place purely with their hands, so fast I can't remember any of it when they are done.

Then he turns to me and says, "Dr. Gaines was one of us."

"What do you mean he was one of you?"

"He was an Illuminatus. Like me, a Servant of the Adepts. Dr. Gaines is the Ninth Prince of the Illuminati."

•

I laugh long and hard at that one.

"Come on, Palmer. He was one of the country's biggest conspiracy nuts until he got locked up. He's the guy who popularized conspiracy. Even normal people buy his book. He's sold something like a million of them. He's a member of the John Birch Society. He's quoted on every conspiracy web site that wants credibility. He hates secret societies."

"Who do you think most of the country's biggest conspiracy theorists are?"

Palmer is smiling at me, that old smile, filled with secrets, that I remember from when we were kids. I say nothing, waiting for him to answer his own question.

He says, "They're ex-Illuminati. That's how they know so much about the Plan."

I stop laughing, clear my throat and say, "You know, Palmer, the problem here is I never know if you're putting me on."

"Give me one good reason why I should kid you, Chad."

"Okay," I say, completely sober now.

"Some other conspiracy theorists are working directly for the Illuminati, and their job is to spread disinformation. Twenty percent of conspiracy-oriented web sites are operated by either the Illuminati or the FBI as a means of surveillance or disseminating disinformation."

My threshold of credulity is lowering; this statement somehow does not surprise me.

"What were you guys talking about then? With your hands, I mean."

"Signs of loyalty, distress and mutual trust," says Gaines, putting on a cardigan sweater he pulled out of his closet, the door covered on the inside and out with newspaper clippings. "We Illuminati don't believe in anything that looks like morality, mind you, but we take our oaths to our brotherhood very seriously, even in self-imposed exile. Palmer was also telling me that he's taken you into his confidence and that we can speak freely in front of you. I have agreed to do so, even though what you learn may get you killed. You're not one of us."

"Thanks, Doc," I say. Just last week, before Jenny left me, he was just another crazy inmate at the asylum who bugged me every day with his nuttiness. Now he's a key to a very real puzzle, and he is no nut after all.

When the world turns upside down on you, it can give you a real headache.

In the Air Force, we call this is a mindfuck.

This doesn't mean, however, that I want to hear him get all smarmy with me. He's still one of my patients and an annoying one at that.

Gaines explains, "When you leave the Illuminati, they often let you be. None of us can keep entirely silent, however. That's why we left. We try to warn the world of what the Illuminati and its many fronts are doing without telling details of what we know about the inside. Like names and faces. If we did that, we would violate our oaths of secrecy."

Palmer chimes in, "We'd experience horrifying deaths, he means to say."

"How do you think the world knows so much about them and what they're doing?" says Gaines. "We tell them, that's why. Or some research-minded individual, turned on by what we tell them, looks at all the books put out by the Illuminati and its fronts, finds a clue here, a clue there, and pieces it all together, right out of the Illuminati's own writings."

"These people are recruited right away for being on the ball," says Palmer.

"Or killed," Gaines says grimly. "The problem is, the more information we put out there, the more the Illuminati seem to enjoy the publicity. Simply by telling the truth, we make ourselves look like wacko cranks and as a result the truth becomes the best smokescreen for them. I guess that's another reason why we're still alive." He suddenly slouches, disgusted. "We are compelled to tell the truth, but in doing so we unwittingly serve the Illuminati Plan. Nothing changes."

"Fubar," Palmer says.

I ask, "How many of you are there now, then, do you think? Runaways or whatever you call them, I mean."

Palmer says, "There have been twenty-six renegades in the past two years. And out of the servants to the thirteen Masters who have defected, I'm lucky thirteen. Now all of us are gone. It will take years to replace us. Those who left but weren't Princes, well, they're dead. So that makes thirteen renegades."

"Dead," I say.

"Dead."

"Christ, Palmer. Seriously, how could you work for these fucking people?"

"Well, to put it real simple, it was fun, Chad. I made a ton of money, and the perks were unbelievable. As a Servant of the Adepts, I was a logistics man, you know, arranged things, which made me powerful. I was also one of the Princes, in line to take over when the Master ahead of me died, and then I'd be a real player in the Game. In the meantime, I had everything I wanted, a huge apartment in Central Park West in Manhattan, unlimited sex with the ten-thousand-dollar-a-night prostitutes that I regularly employed for our work, the whole nine yards. I was the star of my own James Bond movie."

Gaines is grinning at Palmer, his eyes glazed, deep in his private memories.

I can tell that my brother is already missing life on the inside, as Gaines clearly is. As Gaines put it, Palmer is now out of the light.

He smiles. "You know me, Chad, I always hated authority when I was a kid. I was an atheist from the age of four and hated going to church. But I also enjoy authority, you know, that kind of sexy jackboot kind of authority, especially if somebody offers to share some with me. I was seduced. Because that kind of authority isn't authority, it's vision."

"Marvelous," says Gaines. "It was the same for me. As a Prince in the pyramid, I was also a logistics man and had all the same perks. I had more power and money and women than I ever believed possible. But most important, I had access to the mysteries. Secret knowledge passed down for thousands of years."

What is disturbing me at this point is although they are both out of the organization, they're almost wistful about it. I can tell they wish they were back on the inside.

I suddenly feel like I'm at an AA meeting, watching alcoholics lick their lips and talk about getting high.

You can take the guy out of the Illuminati, but you can't take the Illuminati out of the guy, I guess.

"If you worked directly for one of the Masters, do you know who he is?"

"Sure," says Palmer. "So did Dr. Gaines here. He knows who his Master is. Dr. Gaines, please tell my brother Chad about the war. He needs to hear it."

"All right," says Gaines. He adjusts his glasses and strokes his beard. "What you're about to hear, Mr. Carver, is a secret history of western civilization. A part of your brain will reject it violently. Another part will accept it entirely. Are you ready for this conflict in yourself? It could be very harmful to you. Just look at what this secret knowledge did to me."

"Spare me, Doc," I say, "and tell me what the hell is going on. Every day for the past two months, from the first minute you were locked up in here, you've been trying to spill your guts to me and I wouldn't hear a word of it. Don't go frigid on me now that I'm ready to listen. And don't patronize me either."

A manic light shines from Gaines' eyes, piercing the gloom. "So be it."

He tells me about the grand conspiracy of the Illuminati.

I sit on the edge of the bed and open my mind. Then I get this sense of foreboding that it was actually a fair warning; I'm going to be infected with ideas that will change me and my life for the worse. The world, after all, is how you see it from your unique point of view. My point of view, I suddenly believe, is about to wildly change.

And I realize I'm like the kid who has smoked pot but is about to try heroin, and he says to himself, I'll never get hooked on this. I'm in control.

# 11

Rewind two thousand years.

After Jesus was crucified and Christianity, an obscure Judaic sect, began to spread around the Roman Empire and finally became the state religion under the Emperor Constantine, two camps fought for dominance in the early Church.

Gaines tells me that on the one side were the Pauline Christians, descendants of the churches formed by St. Paul, who wrote most of the New Testament. These Christians claimed knowledge of God.

On the other side were the Gnostics, who mixed up Pauline Christianity with their own pagan mystery religions. They claimed direct experience with God, which was called *gnosis* or "illumination."

Usually, one achieved *gnosis* through rituals and arcane symbolic knowledge intended to produce an emotional effect. In the mystery religions, a heavy stimulation of the senses, coupled with symbolism, produced a state of ecstasy and heightened spiritual awareness, during which a god entered you and you became like a god yourself. Music, orgies, incense, drugs and animal and even human sacrifice created the right ambience.

The Gnostics said that heavenly beings had given them secret knowledge, and that these beings would come back to see how they were doing with it. They took this responsibility very seriously. Even back then, these religions were bonafide secret societies.

The early Catholic Church, backed by Constantine, declared its official doctrine at the Council of Nicea, producing the Nicene Creed followed by most churches today. The Empire wasn't big enough for two orthodoxies, so the Church banned Gnosticism; the Pauline Christians, who had for years been persecuted, now persecuted the Gnostics.

The Gnostics, however, had something going for them, which was their longstanding ability to operate in secret.

I tell them, okay, so you had these two religions flourishing in the Roman Empire, the Catholic state religion and an underground Gnostic religion that, as far as I could tell, represented the combined wisdom of most of the Roman Empire's greatest nuts.

Gaines says, "A core group of Gnostics called themselves the Illuminati."

Ah, I say, suddenly enlightened.

Palmer adds, "This next part might sound a little freaky to you, Chad. See, Gnostics worship the Light-Bringer, the giver of secret knowledge and enlightenment. The Light-Bringer has many counterparts in various pagan religions, such as Ormuzd and Osiris. In the Christian religion, this deity is Lucifer. Lucifer, after all, gave to mankind the fruits of the Tree of Knowledge of Good and Evil in the Garden of Eden—the gift of illumination— then conspired with Adam and Eve to keep it secret from God."

"Satan," I say, fighting the urge to spit. "You're talking about Satan. The Gnostics think Satan is the real God."

"Yeah," says Palmer.

My brother, the reformed Satanist.

"So where does the real God fit in? You know, the God of Christianity?"

Gaines tells me, "Jehovah exists, but he is called the *panurgia* and considered a primal insane force that created the physical universe, or realm of darkness. The loving, caring God is Lucifer, the bringer of light, or Truth, who exists not in the material plane but one of pure spirit, or light. Properly illuminated, a man can transcend the material plane and become spirit himself. To the Gnostics, Jesus was this guy who had figured out how to be a god; that's why he told his disciples that he spoke in parables so that only a select group of followers would understand these 'mysteries hidden since the foundation of the world.'"

Gaines lights a cigarette and drags on it heavily.

"The opposing sides had been defined," he says. "War had been declared. Now it would begin in earnest."

•

The Roman Empire fell.

The Church converted the barbarians and exerted control over them by granting divine right to kings. As the Middle Ages continued, the Illuminati infiltrated groups that met in secret, such as the stonemason guilds, who became the Freemasons of today. They also got into banking and business, realizing that money, not the sword, meant power. Since Christians at the time could not loan money to make interest, the Illuminati recruited Jews.

Gaines tells me that no Jewish conspiracy to take over the world exists. Most of the Illuminati are not Jews. *The Protocols of the Elders of Zion* was a bad forgery. But the Illuminati needed Jews to do banking, and so Jews were recruited.

When the Crusades came and the Christian army took Jerusalem, a group of men gained permission from the King of Jerusalem to found the Knights Templar, a religious military order, and stationed themselves in the ruins of Solomon's Temple. While their soldiers fought the Moslems, the Illuminati leaders of the Knights Templar made connections with Oriental secret societies such as the Assassins, a fanatical Islamic sect and the followers of one Hasan bin Sabah, whose famous motto was, "Nothing is true. Everything is permissible."

It's from Hasan bin Sabah's name that we get the word "assassin" as well as "hashish," as his followers smoked tons of dope before they went out and killed the leaders of their enemies. An Assassin would be sent out to serve in a foreign government. A few years or even decades later he would get a signal, then stab to death the foreign king, caliph, sheik, whatever, in his own bed. From the Assassins, the Illuminati learned the fine art of assassination and realized that wars could be won through killing the enemy's leader.

The Knights Templar grew rich, powerful and prestigious. They were granted immense lands in many countries and the Pope favored them for a time. They were the world's first international corporation. The Illuminati had finally begun to operate out in the open. Years later, however, the Pope declared the Knights Templar to be heretics and the King of France massacred them. The King had simply wanted to get out of debt, but the Pope knew that the Templars were a dangerous cult and an enemy of the Church.

It was discovered, for example, that in one Templar ceremony, you spat on the Cross and in another, you worshipped a god called Baphomet, represented by a big wooden penis or an image of a cat. The Templars also practiced magic and were into weird sex.

The Church finally caught on that something big was going on right under their noses and declared war on Gnostics of all stripes. The Pope founded the Jesuit Order to root out and destroy them. The entire Inquisition, in fact, was the Church's response to the threat created by this paganism that refused to go away, once it finally realized that it was indeed at war.

One of the Crusades never made it into the Holy Land, for example, but instead marched into southern France to exterminate the Cathari heresy.

Again, the Illuminati returned to their power base in Freemasonry and other secretive organizations. After the Templar experience, they became determined to undermine the monarchies because they believed that since kingships were confirmed by the Church, they would always, ultimately, be enemies. The enlightened should rule, they believed, not kings. Both Church and State should be overthrown and destroyed.

In defeat, the Illuminati only became more ambitious and dangerous.

Never again would they operate in the open, nor would they challenge the Church except in small attacks over centuries until they grew powerful enough to crush it altogether.

During the Age of Enlightenment, however, the Illuminati felt strong enough to launch a major attack. Their plans culminated in the French Revolution, American Revolution and other revolutions against the European monarchies.

"Liberty, equality and fraternity" was practically a Freemason slogan.

Engineering two major revolutions gave them a real taste for power and showed them what they could accomplish with organization, money and secrecy. They learned that people were easy to stir up to rebel against centralized authority, and that they were easily duped. Their goal became world government to establish the New World Order.

In the New World Order, Christianity and private property will be abolished under a dictatorship of the enlightened until everybody becomes enlightened, at which time the dictatorship will wither away.

If that sounds like Communism, be assured it's not a coincidence. The Illuminati also engineered the Bolshevik Revolution of 1918, one of their blunders.

Some other Illuminati's experiments and plans backfired or got out of hand, such as recruiting Hitler as a Master and World War II. They constantly experimented as they progressed. They even dabbled with cultural revolution by encouraging the psychedelic '60s movement, using the CIA to distribute LSD to America's restless youth, and later the New Age movement that got so big in the '80s. Later, they founded the Council on Foreign Relations, the Trilateral Commission and the Bilderbergers so that they could use the top minds in the world as a think tank on how to achieve their plans, which is world government. These think tanks turned all these influential people, a veritable Who's Who of government, industry and media, into unwitting collaborators.

For the Illuminati, the end justifies the means. There is no absolute morality for them. They will do anything and everything, including lying, murder, massacre—anything—to fulfill their Plan of world domination.

To take over the world over a period of about a thousand years, you first take a nation state and make it democratic so that you can separate Church and State, and so that its leader is a common citizen chosen by the people rather than a king chosen by blood.

You also weaken belief in Christianity by ridiculing it in the media and promoting magic and other Gnostic concepts to make them acceptable, even attractive, in pop culture. You create dependence on your organization through debt and blackmail. You confuse your enemies by creating front organizations, some benign, some outright scary—in any case, all a smokescreen. You attract new blood into your organization by offering clues in a proliferation of confusing works produced by these front organizations. Your would-be enemies are also admirers; every conspiracy theorist has a secret longing to be on the inside.

You create an atmosphere of fear and disorder that make common people want more security. You create situations of terror that make these people willingly give up their freedom piece by piece.

Once you do all that, you get your man in charge, he becomes dictator, and that's it.

Gaines tells me that this is how we got the Great Seal of the United States, which Roosevelt put on the back of the dollar bill by executive order. Part of the Great Seal is the eagle, but the other part is a pyramid with thirteen steps leading up to the illuminated "All-Seeing Eye of God." The thirteen steps, of course, represent the thirteen Masters of the Illuminati.

The goal of achieving the New World Order is printed on the back of the one-dollar bill, in Latin words framing the Great Seal of the United States.

*Annuit coeptis novus ordo seclorum.*

This means, "Announcing the Birth of the New Order of the Ages."

•

Instead of exhausting me, all of this new information is exhilarating me, filling me with energy. This is like watching a movie, and I want to hear about the good guys.

"So where does the Catholic Church fit in?" I ask them.

Palmer says, "Remember all those Catholic assassins and would-be assassins I was telling you about earlier today?"

I tell him yes. They killed Garfield and McKinley and tried to kill a few other presidents, or so the theory goes.

"That's where the Church fits in," Palmer says. "That's their work. Not the Church itself, remember, but a secret element in the Church, a special branch of the Jesuits designed to fight the Illuminati. They killed Woodrow Wilson because he handed control of America's money supply to rich men controlled by the Illuminati. Their secret assassination unit is even better than the CIA's Division-5. Yes, you could say they're the good guys, meaning they're not trying to turn the world into a big concentration camp. Their methods, however, are just as savage as the Illuminati's. You have to fight fire with fire. But they're losing their grip inch by inch, yard by yard. Consider the Reformation. Communism. Charles Darwin. The revival of the New Age movement. The decline of religion in America. Constant ridicule in movies and the press. Name one movie where Catholics or Catholic priests are depicted fairly. Anyway, back to the big picture. The problem with the Church is that it's right out there in the open—it's big and slow and can be easily attacked. For all the ruthlessness of the Jesuits' counter-Illuminati forces, it's hard to fight the Illuminati. Since the Illuminati can operate in secret, the Church can only react and countermove. The Illuminati always have the initiative. In any game, initiative means victory."

Palmer pauses and lights up one of Gaines' cigarettes.

"I've been dying for one of these," he says, sighing. "I guess quitting smoking was a bad idea the week I decided to betray the Illuminati."

Despite everything I've heard, I laugh at that.

Palmer and Gaines don't laugh. Gaines lights up his own cigarette. He's smoking his unfiltered Camels like a chimney, constantly spitting tobacco from his lips. The room fills with smoke. Suddenly I feel like a conspirator myself.

Palmer says, "Seriously, Chad, you know the Book of Revelation in the Bible, the coming of the Antichrist, and all that stuff? Well, that's the world the Illuminati are going to create. They will promise a world of magic and illumination, where 'do what thou wilt shall be the whole of the law.' Free love and extra fluoride in the water and LSD sold next to the M&Ms at convenience stores. They say they want to redefine reality, get all of man to become Superman. Men will be taught to be as gods in an enlightened humanist paradise."

He says, "But what they will deliver is going to be more like George Orwell's *1984.*"

Gaines chimes in and tells me that after the Illuminati take over the United States these laws will be passed: Government inspection of your mail. Electronic surveillance in all public places. Elimination of private ownership of guns. Travel restrictions. Complete censorship of all media. Cops stopping and frisking you at will, breaking down your door for a search without a warrant or probable cause. Automatic filing on all citizens in a national database, including DNA sample and fingerprinting. Elimination of private property. Government seizure of the means of production. Repeal of the tax-exempt status, then destruction, of all churches. Transfer of all money to a centralized computer credit system. Loyalty oaths, followed by barcode tattoos on all citizens. Eugenics programs designed to favor people with higher IQs. Sterilization of people with unfavorable genes.

The Illuminati are already setting up concentration camps to house dissidents. In fact, he says, there are twenty-three large detention camps already in existence in the United States, created by FEMA, that can house about seven hundred thousand people. The biggest one is an underground camp outside of Denver and has its own airport.

Gaines tells me that there is a law, granted by Presidential Executive Order, that grants the government, notably the President, FEMA and the Attorney General, many of these powers, to be used in the event of a national emergency. Under the War Powers Act, the President can declare a national emergency at any time; all he has to do is notify Congress and publish it in the *Federal Register*. Most modern Presidents declare at least one or two hundred national emergencies during their administrations. Jackson himself declared seventy-three.

A large-scale blackout, he says, with subsequent looting and anarchy, would easily justify declaring a new national emergency and invoking existing law to deny freedoms guaranteed by the Constitution.

Gaines is smiling. The architecture for creating a totalitarian state is all there in existing U.S law, for everyone to see, he says.

"Jesus Christ," I say. "And Congress knows about this?"

"Of course they do."

"Why don't they stop it?"

Gaines is still smiling. "This is America. Dictatorship can't happen here."

"So why did you guys leave them? You, Palmer, you worked for them for fifteen years, since you were a teenager. You must have known what their goals were all along. Why did you suddenly decide to leave now?"

This is a serious question. Me, I'm actually thinking at this point that I would rather be on their side. They seem to have all the cards.

Palmer smokes his cigarette, frowning.

He says, "They're real close, Chad. This great economy we've got, the security we have, well, it's all going down the drain. The Illuminati are ready for their next experiment. They are going to slowly push the United States and see how far they can get before people cry out to have the Constitution shredded even further until it barely exists. This will include terrorism, blackouts, disinformation campaigns and a thousand other dirty tricks that would make you puke to hear about. The Oklahoma City bombing, that TWA plane going down and the Waco siege were just test runs for the big push. If they succeed, the time will be ripe for the dictator."

"Shit," I say seriously.

He grinds out his cigarette into one of Gaines' overflowing ashtrays.

Gaines says, "I was seduced as Palmer was, but as you can see, I gave it all up to fight them. They're going too far. We always thought we could enjoy life on the inside for our entire lives, following orders, giving orders and never actually seeing the world crushed. But the present Masters are impatient. They want to step up the pace. The world is their chessboard. They say all the new technologies out there, like the Internet, enable us to accelerate the Plan's schedule. They're going to make it happen now. They're going too far. That's why every one of the Princes left the Illuminati over the past two years."

Palmer frowns as he pulls another cigarette out of Gaines' pack. "Yes. You're right about that. They're going too far."

"And we're going to stop them," I say, prompting him. "Right?"

Palmer cups his hands as he lights the tip of the cigarette.

He winces through a cloud of smoke and says, "Yeah, Chad. That's a great idea. And exactly how the fuck are we ever going to do that?"

# 12

Martin Dobbs sees me coming out of Gaines' room and I'm caught red-handed, while Palmer does a disappearing act.

"I'm glad you decided to come in," says Dobbs. "I need to see you in my office."

That's where he sits me down and tells me that I'm out of a job.

Congress passed that damn Medicare Law, he says, and the County is trying to tighten its belt. He squints under the glare of the overhead fluorescent lights.

My head is buzzing and I'm thinking, my life is out of control.

Given the new information I've received today, however, I'm wondering if it ever was in control. I'm thinking about how having a wife, a job and money gives you the illusion of control, but you never really have it.

Even lighting has control over you.

At work, the lights are bright and cold white fluorescents, designed to make you sharp and ready for work.

At home, the lights are warm orange incandescents, designed to make you feel cozy and relaxed.

You can't let me go, I tell Dobbs. Next week is Family Week. You'll need me.

Dobbs has a good heart. He spreads his hands over his desk in a helpless gesture.

I'm just following orders, he says. There are cutbacks.

Dobbs' walls are gray. All of the walls of the institution are gray. Gray is psychologically a neutral color, but we have a pink room where we put patients who are acting out.

I'm real sorry, Dobbs says in his gravelly voice.

He says, you need a break anyway, don't you think there, Chad?

You look exhausted.

You look like you're about to snap.

You look like you've got a steel spring up your ass.

I'm sitting here thinking that everything around us is designed to affect us emotionally. Not just lighting and color, but everything. Ergonomic office spaces. Architecture and design. Advertising that makes you want and need stuff you don't really want or need. You feel like you define yourself by the type of car you drive.

Me, I drive a truck, which makes me a rugged small town type.

When Jenny and I were to finally get around to having kids, we were going to get a minivan. That would mark me as a family man.

It's all a type of mind control.

I'm crossing another line, I can tell. Creeping bullshit. Except instead of buying more of Palmer's bullshit, though, this time I'm making up my own. Thinking creatively about it. Making my own connections.

Our little meeting with Gaines has thoroughly messed me up.

Dobbs says, you need a rest, Chad.

He wants to know when was the last time I got a good night's sleep.

He wants to know if I'm taking any medication.

He wants to know how things are going at home.

I tell myself I'm okay, though, because I don't believe a vast intelligence is behind the forms of mind control that go on in America.

Not yet, anyway.

The explanation is that people have ancient biological needs to get sex, status and immorality and other people, knowing that, create products and marketing to satisfy those needs. It's that simple.

Dobbs tells me that he's going to miss me around the hospital, and that the patients will surely feel the same way, too.

I am thinking, however, about the synchronicity involved in me losing my job. I learn about the Illuminati and just two days later I lose my job. I was ready to leave it to maybe go back to school anyway, but it sure is strange.

I find myself wondering if the Illuminati are giving me a warning. Telling me that they control everything. I don't want to think this, but I can't help myself.

•

During the drive home, Palmer tells me that it's good that I lost the job.

"You can't tell anybody what you learned today," he says. "You'll endanger yourself and them both. And the less you leave the house, at least for a while, the better. Gaines said the Illuminati basically leave the renegades alone, but I do know about the blackout. That might make me dangerous to them, I don't know. After the blackout, though, I think we'll be safe. You can go back to school or do whatever it is you want to do. I've got money. Then I'll get out of your hair or whatever you want. I just need a place to stay for a while."

I grunt, focusing on the road. My mind is in pieces. I can't think about the future right now.

He says, "Put your seat belt on, Chad."

I pull on the belt while I drive. "So how are they going to do it? The blackout?"

"They're going to use the Pentagon's forty-million-dollar High-Frequency Active Auroral Research Program, or HAARP for short. They built a hundred and eighty towers up in Alaska about two hundred miles outside of Anchorage. The towers are used to cook the Earth's ionosphere, making it the world's largest transmitter so that bases on the ground can talk to subs that are far underwater. It will be used in conjunction with GWEN, the Ground Wave Emergency Network, an '80s government project that built towers all the way across the United States that are three hundred feet tall and broadcast pulses of electromagnetic radiation as low-frequency messages. GWEN was developed so that in case of a nuclear war or something, the government can still function. Anyway, the science involved here is an old dream of Nikola Tesla, that crazy inventor whose patents made it possible for us to use AC in addition to DC power and also use the radio, which he invented before Marconi. Tesla used to talk about using the wireless transmission of energy as a death ray. That's how TWA Flight 800 went down back in '96—electromagnetic radiation beamed at it. Using the system as an incredible weapon is the secret aim of these government projects, but that doesn't mean the Illuminati, using its connections, can't borrow it for this special purpose right under the Army's nose."

"I don't understand a single word of what you just said, but I take it that we won't be able to stop the Illuminati by going after their means of cutting the power."

"Not unless we go to Alaska and blow up some towers, which are heavily guarded."

"It just gets weirder and weirder," I say. "What a weird fucking day."

He eyes me curiously. "So how do you feel?"

"Paranoid as hell."

"Good."

"I'm waking up. I feel like I'm awake. Reborn."

"That's a good thing."

"I'm not so sure about that, Jesus. Ignorance is bliss, you know. I wasn't real happy with my life, but I sure was comfortable. Now I look at everything like a skeptic. I look for a hidden agenda in everything I see. Everything has to be interpreted."

"'Doubt is the beginning of wisdom.' Clarence Darrow."

"It's exhausting. Before, the Establishment made it so that I'm powerless, and now I see what's going on, but I'm still powerless." I sigh loudly. "Christ, I miss Jenny."

I feel completely alone. Palmer is all I have right now.

He nods, silent.

I say, "I'm not sure whether I should thank you or punch you."

Palmer says quietly, "Would you rather I had left you out of all this?"

After a few moments, I answer him: "I guess not."

"I'm in the same boat as you. Look at me. I can predict a power outage in which a hundred thousand casualties are predicted by a computer, and nobody but you believes me. Then after that, I'm out. I don't know what their next move will be. All I'll know is what I told you, which is just an echo of what every other conspiracy crank is saying. I'll be your average conspiracy freak, like Hiram Gaines. Like you said, it'll just be more noise."

"Which, like he said, discredits the truth and makes a perfect smokescreen for them."

Palmer sags under his seat belt. "We're doomed, then. All of us. And they will win."

We drive in silence for a while. It's hard for me to imagine Fox Mulder on *The X-Files* actually unwittingly helping Cigarette Man and the bad guys. Then I remember that this isn't a TV show. So I try to think of the opposite of what Fox Mulder would do. Fox Mulder's actions, after all, are written by guys who want another season for the *The X-Files*. We don't want another season.

I get this incredible flash of insight.

"Hey Palmer, you said you know one of the Masters, right?"

"Sure. I was a Prince. I worked directly for him. But I can't tell you his name."

"Okay. Gaines also worked for one of them, though. He was a Prince, too."

"Yeah. I can tell you that all of them are presently living in the United States. There are four in the New York City area. That's where I was living for all these years, under a different name. The guy I worked for actually doesn't live that far from here."

"And these Illuminati, they're just people."

"That's one thing you should always remember. It'll keep you from freaking out, Chad. They eat, sleep, shit and screw just like everybody else."

"That means they can also die."

Palmer eyes me curiously. "Of course. What are you getting at?"

"What I'm getting at," I say, "is that we should kill the motherfuckers. Then there will be no blackout. Or if there is, at least it will be their last gasp."

"And how do we. . . ? Oh."

"That's right. We set up our own conspiracy."

Palmer is catching on, perking up. "That's a hell of an idea, Chad. We get all the Princes together and make each of them responsible for killing one of the Masters."

"Then there will be no more Illuminati," I say grimly.

He sighs and says, "If only we could trust each other."

I nod. "Gaines kept looking at you like he wasn't sure if you were a defector or an infiltrator. I think he decided each time that it didn't matter either way. It didn't matter to him."

"Now you're understanding how weird this conspiracy is," says Palmer. "I hardly know who I am myself anymore. I feel cut off from everything I know. I operated in a world of secrets for fifteen years. And I don't know if I've been conditioned. A lot of what I know is what they told me. Since they're liars, I really don't know anything."

"You knew that the President was going to be shot. That was good enough for me." I look at my brother. "I believe you, Palmer. At least the part about the blackout. If we can't go to the cops or the FBI or somebody, then that's reason enough to kill them ourselves."

"It'd be hard as hell, Chad. Their houses are like fortresses, and they rarely leave them to go anywhere. Each assassination would have to be public. With a rifle, at a distance. Tricky work. The target is usually mobile and that makes it real tricky. Better to use a pistol up close, but then the assassin will be at best arrested and at worst, killed on the spot."

I chew on the insides of my mouth, considering this.

He says, "We have to get them when they're all leaving their houses at the same time. Maybe to go to a meeting. But the meetings are secret. They track our movements, too. The Princes, I mean. We could never even get close. We'd be dogmeat. Not to pass the buck, but—"

"But somebody else has to do it," I say.

"If it was at all possible, then yes, somebody else has to do it."

I'm thinking that person might have to be me. I can do Palmer's boss, and Gaines can find somebody to kill his boss, and so on until all thirteen are dead. Nice and simple. The Illuminati conspiracy would be stopped and a hundred thousand people would be saved. America—the world, actually—would be saved from terror and dictatorship.

Or so the theory goes.

He says, "Nobody's ever tried it before in their history. To kill the Masters all at once. Nobody's gotten that close. But that strength may be their weakness."

If only I pull the trigger, and twelve other guys just like me do the same.

Nice and simple.

This fact fills me with sudden terror.

At the same time, I feel free, excited. The idea gives me a sense of control.

Fool's courage. I'd never do it and I know it.

Would you throw yourself on a grenade to save your comrades? Maybe you would.

But would you throw yourself on a grenade to save your comrades if you knew, after your death, you would be called a nut who pulled the pin on the grenade in the first place?

I'd end up killing some old guy who has a family, go to jail, and wonder for the rest of my life behind bars if I really did prevent the blackout and save the world, if it was all real or just this feverish dream. A part of me is still thinking this can't be real, that it's this giant put-on.

One of the first symptoms of paranoid schizophrenia is delusions of grandeur.

Another is to see vast conspiracies that involve governments, business, the media, Satanic secret societies, and you starring in a lead role.

I watched the President get killed after my brother predicted it. I heard a lot of weird conspiracy theories today, parts of which I've already heard from various schizophrenics and other assorted nuts. To tell the truth, I'm still getting a really good cheap thrill from all this. Like an addict, it makes me only crave more information so that I can keep this twisted high and keep my mind, hopefully forever, off of my wife's absence.

Getting personally involved, however, does sober you up.

What a mindfuck, I think to myself.

When we get home and pull into my driveway, three hard-looking men in black are waiting on the front porch. Palmer and I stare at them in quiet fear as I slow the truck to a crawl. Out of the corner of my eye, I can see Palmer trembling.

"Fuck me," I say. "There really are 'men in black.'"

They know about us and our plot already. They're that good.

Or maybe Gaines ratted us out somehow.

In any case, we're dead men.

Adrenaline is rushing like electricity through my body and for the first time, I realize I'm not watching a movie, I'm directly involved and I could die as the price of that involvement.

Palmer fidgets in his seat. He seems to be trying to decide if he should give me the order to throw the car into reverse, step on the gas and make a run for it.

I'm not going to wait for him to make up his mind. I'm getting us the hell out of here.

Then I see the men more clearly, and realize that they are Catholic priests.

# 13

The Catholic Church is the largest organization of Christians in the world with more than a billion members who believe that the bishop of Rome, the Pope, has the highest authority in matters of Christian faith.

The Catholics believe that the Pope is the inheritor of the powers and commission that Jesus gave to the twelve Apostles.

The word "Catholic" comes from a Greek word that means, "universal."

The Church is based on a pyramidal power structure starting with dioceses, headed by bishops, who preside over parishes and their attendant clergy. Above the bishops are the cardinals who make up the Supreme Council of the Church, which elects the Pope. And above the cardinals is the Pope himself, whose decisions are inspired directly by God, Christ and the Holy Ghost.

It is believed that the Catholic religious ritual is a mystery, and that the Holy Ghost is always present in the Church.

Also operating under the Pope are two other power structures, the *curia* and the orders. The *curia* is a bureaucracy housed in Vatican City that reports to the Secretariat of State of this tiny country, who in turn works for the Pope. The orders are brotherhoods and sisterhoods founded to study the Bible and provide charitable services to the poor, including food distribution, education and healthcare.

These orders include the Paulist Fathers, Dominicans, Carmelites, Franciscans, Legion of Christ, Benedictines, Marianists, Salesians and Jesuits, among others.

In the Church's raw beginnings, all of the churches of the Roman world united under the Emperor Constantine, swore allegiance to the Bishop of Rome and then declared the Church's official doctrine at the Council of Nicea in 325 A.D. After that, all Christian sects who disagreed with that official doctrine, or "heresies," were suppressed.

Among these were the Gnostics. Many of them were persecuted.

In the Middle Ages, Inquisitions were set up to destroy the Cathari and Waldenses heresies; in fact, one of the Crusades did not go to the Holy Land at all, but instead went into the region of Languedoc in southern France for the purpose of exterminating the Cathari, which was accomplished.

Some people believe that the Cathari were wiped because they had documents proving that the Holy Grail, carrying the blood and body of Christ, was actually Jesus himself, or Mary Magdalene, carrying Jesus' child, and that this lineage can be connected to the Merengovian Dynasty in southern France.

Between 1307 and 1314, the French government tortured and executed all members of the Order of the Knights Templar. In 1314, Jacques de Molay, the leader of the knights, who had been arrested seven years earlier on Friday the Thirteenth, was burned at the stake.

In 1478, the Spanish Inquisition began, run by Dominican and Franciscan friars with their own bureaucracies, and backed by the Spanish crown. The Inquisitors tried the accused and the government killed them when they were found guilty and unrepentant, which was quite often. Converted Jews and Moslems, mostly, were persecuted and many of them were burned at the stake, their property confiscated. Illuminati members, or illuminists or Alumbrados as they were called in Spain, were the real target. Thousands died.

The Society of Jesus was founded in 1540 in Spain by St. Ignatius of Loyola, while the Inquisition was in full swing.

Later on, during the Protestant Reformation, with cooperation between Church and State eroding throughout Europe in persecuting heretics such as the Gnostics, a group of fanatical Jesuits, called the Black Popes, formed to covertly fight the tide of Protestantism and the Illuminati. Their agents fanned out across Europe, murdering Protestant royalty and Gnostics and spreading Catholicism. It was believed that the Black Popes had tried to assassinate Henry III, Henry IV and Elizabeth I.

Palmer told me that the activities of the Black Popes never ended. Fanatical Jesuits and elements of the Pope's Swiss Guard today make up an ultrasecret counter-Illuminati group called the *Soldati di Christ*, or Christian Soldiers.

He said that the Christian Soldiers killed John Paul I, one of their own Popes, because they suspected him of being an agent of the Illuminati bent on liberalizing the Church.

Today, there are more than twenty-two thousand Jesuits in active ministries around the globe. It is the largest order of the Roman Catholic Church.

Almost nobody knows about the Christian Soldiers, however, Palmer told me. It is a secret group that has operated within the Church for centuries, protecting it, internally and externally, from the Illuminati.

•

After I park the truck, Palmer asks me, "Do you have your gun on you?"

"No. Anyhow, do you really think I'm going to shoot a Catholic priest in broad daylight on my porch?"

Palmer sighs and opens his door.

"All right. Let's just hope those nice Jesuits don't shoot us. Remember that to them, I'm the enemy. And that makes you the enemy. Stay close and be cool."

One of the priests spreads his hands in welcome as we approach.

*"Li significhiamo nessun danno. Siamo venuto nella pace. Desideriamo semplicemente comunicare con voi. E quello accettable?"*

I don't speak Italian, but at least he sounds friendly.

Then I remember Palmer telling me how you get killed in this game—with a smile in front of you and a gun pointed at the back of your head.

The friendly priest is an older man, around fifty years old, with a thin face and spooky Mediterranean-blue eyes. A shock of white hair falls over his forehead, which he sweeps back with his hand. The men on either side of him are of a harder sort. They do not smile. They have the blank, shining stare of fanatics. One is a short Sicilian with a crewcut, a clean-shaven square jaw and eyes that look like black marbles. The other looks Swiss, with blond hair longer than Palmer's and eyes the color of flint.

The Swiss is holding a briefcase.

Palmer grins up at them from the bottom of the porch steps, squinting against the sun, and says in what sounds like German, *"Willkomen zu unserem wenig Haus, Vater."*

The priest's face twitches, his smile gone. *"Dovete parlare quel linguaggio horrid, Illuminato? Parliamo il linguaggio di questo paese. Americano, se voi per favore."*

"All right," says Palmer, eyeing the briefcase, "we'll speak American. So you say you are here in peace. Let's head inside and have a chat."

As we go into the house, Palmer sings, "Onward, Christian Soldiers. . . ."

The Sicilian stares at me icily as if I'm the one making fun of them.

We sit in my living room and I awkwardly ask everybody if they want a beer, which is declined. The Jesuits sit on the couch together, keeping their coats on, fists clenched on their laps. I grab a chair from the kitchen and park myself outside of their little circle. Around us are the paraphernalia of my years with Jenny—pictures of us on the walls, a big framed wedding photo over the fireplace, little knickknacks that took years for her to collect at flea markets.

This is my home, and suddenly I'm a stranger in it.

Palmer makes himself comfortable on the recliner, lights one of Gaines' cigarettes out of a pack that he swiped, and says pleasantly, "Well, this is certainly an unexpected visit, *Vater*. I didn't know you guys were so good. I guess it doesn't pay to underestimate your adversary in the Game."

The old priest smiles politely at the compliment.

Me, I'm stupidly thinking that Jenny doesn't like smoking in the house.

"You already know who I am, I presume," Palmer says.

The priest nods. "*Tredicesimo Principe del Illuminato. Tredicesimo Servo Dei Adepts.* Seems I'm in the presence of royalty, and a bit of a legend in the Game."

"You're too kind, *Vater*. And you know that this is my brother, Chad Carver."

The priest looks at me with a mixture of pity and disgust.

"Yes, we know who he is," he says. "He's nobody."

I raise my eyebrows, but keep my mouth shut.

I'm bigger than all of these men, but right now I'm feeling powerless.

"And you are. . . .?" Palmer says, keeping it pleasant.

"You can call me John or Father, as you've been doing. As for my brethren, you can call him Irenaeus and him Hippolytus."

"This is exciting," Palmer says, pulling up his legs so that he sits cross-legged. "Real-live *Cristiani Soldati.* Servants of the Black Popes. I've never met one of you guys in the flesh."

"You have defected," John says. "You are exposed. Are you ready to accept Jesus Christ as your savior and repent your sins? Some of you *Illuminato* have. As I'm sure you're aware, they became fundamentalists—not our people, granted, but on the same side, nonetheless. They receive our Holy Father's protection as they go out and preach against the *Illuminato*."

"Sure, I'll accept Jesus," says Palmer. "What else do you want while you're here?"

"Well, I should think that any information you might have would certainly be helpful, if relevant to our cause, now that we are all Christians in this room. Such as the names of any *Illuminato* agents in the Society of Jesus." The priest's face twitches. "It might demonstrate your faith to do your first good works."

"I might just do that. Help you, I mean. But since my new faith hasn't really had time to take root yet, what are you offering?"

John stands up, brushes off his pant legs casually, and smiles at me. He starts fiddling with a ring he wears on his left hand.

"Chad Jonathan Carver. You're not a church-goer and unfortunately you're not one of our flock, but you do call yourself a Christian. A Lutheran, to be exact, which is not so distant a cousin from the divinely inspired doctrines of our mother Church as one might assume. Your last visit to church was four years ago."

Startled, I say, "That's right."

"Do you need any spiritual counseling while we're here? I understand, and do regret, that your wife has disappeared. Hippolytus is an excellent minister and a superb healer."

I return the Sicilian's frosty stare for a few moments, swallow hard and say, "No, thanks."

I try to tell myself that these are the good guys.

"Splendid. The Holy Ghost is in this house. As a fellow Christian, I'd like to ask you a question. Your brother served Satan for fourteen years. How does that make you feel?"

I resented him brushing me aside at the start of this *Gong Show* but now I'd like nothing better than to be left alone. I feel like the kid cornered by his math teacher for a pop quiz in front of the entire class.

I tell him, "Well, he says he's done with all that now."

"The Gnostics, the Knowing Ones as they are called, among other things, are worshippers of Satan. They are our mutual enemy, Mr. Carver. The Catholic Church has always operated out in the open, while they skulk in the dark. Did you know that there were several brands of Gnostic exegesis, not just one? You do not have the advantage of a higher education, but you do read a lot of books. History, I believe, is one of your favorite subjects. One branch of Gnosticism believed that since the spirit and the body are separate, then whatever you do with the body, including licentiousness, adultery and murder, does not matter. Other Gnostics said that murder is good, because the greater the sin, the greater the forgiveness God gets to bestow upon the sinner. Others believed that God is the *Demiurge*, or a blind insane creator that made the physical universe, a prison that separates us as spiritual beings from the one true God of the spirit, who is Lucifer. Ormazd. Satan. Still others believed that the Serpent had intercourse with Eve and fathered Cain, which is why the human anatomy has serpentine intestines.

"They all held one thing in common, however, besides a love for evil. In fact, they maintain these beliefs to this very day: They believe that eating the apple from the Tree of Knowledge of Good and Evil was not the Original Sin that resulted in the fall from Heavenly Grace, but an act of liberation, as secret knowledge leads mankind back to the light, the realm of the spirit. The Sodomites, Cain, Judas Iscariot and Lucifer are the true inheritors of the Kingdom of God that will come, not you or me or any other Christian. They say that to love Christ is to accept slavery and never be as gods ourselves. They maintain that morality, as in basic right and wrong, is a matter of human opinion, not given to us as an absolute from the one true God. They steal our holy traditions but reverse the values. They borrow our churchly clothes but they are still wolves under them. Evil is good to their like, and good is evil. These are the *Illuminato's* most cherished beliefs, Mr. Carver."

Palmer says, playing the smartass, "You're hurting my feelings over here, *Vater*."

John stares into my eyes and says, "These teachings were, and are, *didaskalias daimonion*, things taught by demons. The actions of the *Illuminato* are the same as demons. *Libera me Domine*! They live on the bitter poison of the serpent and are the authors of all apostasy."

He turns and points at Palmer.

"Your brother was one of them. He believed it all. He was not an unwitting stooge, as you clearly are, Mr. Carver. He was *Principe* in their ranks. *Tredicesimo Principe del Illuminato*. Simon Magus. Servant to the Grand Sovereign Master of all the *Illuminato* and heir to the throne of the Masters of the World. He hates them now for some reason—that I believe. But do you really think he has ever stopped loving the devil?"

I want to say that the priest is pushing it too far and acting like a religious nut, but he's kind of making a good point.

What I do believe, and want to tell him, is that I don't think Palmer believes in anything, God or the devil.

"Can you leave my brother out of it?" Palmer says. He looks disgusted. "This is juvenile."

"Why, *Principe*? I'm simply telling our side of the story to a fellow Christian. A man who is my brother. Is there something that we have in common that we can talk about?"

"Yeah. I'd like to do a deal. No fooling."

"Do tell. I'm listening."

"Let me say first that your people have always been a noble and worthy adversary, *Vater*, but you were my enemy and old habits die hard. So I'm not signing up with you in any way, shape or form. I'm sure you're not excited about the prospect of letting me anywhere near inside your organization either. But I'd like to call us allies depending on what you bring to the table. The Illuminati are my enemy and I have a plan to do something about them."

John glances at me, then says, "This is most intriguing. Perhaps there is a place we can speak privately."

"We can go upstairs. That all right with you, Chad?"

I nod, grateful to get rid of them. "Sure."

The priest says wearily, "I do hope you're going to tell me that you plan to do something more interesting than write a book or start a web site."

Palmer gets up and leads the priest up the stairs, followed by Irenaeus, who has the briefcase, and I'm left with Hippolytus, who stares at me with cold-blooded murder in his eyes.

He looks like the kind of guy who, if he has a choice of killing you with a gun or his bare hands, will choose his bare hands every time.

I wonder how many people he has killed for Christ.

At the same time, I can feel myself crossing another line of creeping bullshit. Except it's not creeping anymore. I'm being thrown in headfirst. The priests showing up broke down what I think was my final layer of resistance to all weirdness.

The real world, or what I thought was the real world, is now somewhere behind me.

It's not completely gone, I know that. But it's like I'm orbiting it.

After about twenty minutes of staring at me, Hippolytus says, "Sorry about your wife."

"Thanks," I tell him.

"Do you want to talk about it? Perhaps we could pray together."

"No. Thank you."

We return to our uncomfortable silence, which lasts another hour.

Outside, it's dark. Upstairs, Palmer and Father John are doing a deal.

Conspiracies, like politics, make strange bedfellows.

This is how we get the rifles, ammunition, espionage equipment and a cool two hundred and fifty thousand dollars in cash.

# Part Three

112                                          *Craig DiLouie*

# 14

Five days until the power goes out.

This morning, two guys in a truck dropped off fifteen crates labeled 'Medical Supplies.'

They put the crates in my basement, tracking leaves into the house, and then left without getting a signature.

After Palmer does a sweep and cleans out the bugs the Christian Soldiers dropped around the house and put in the crates, he opens one up with a knife and pulls out the components of some type of rifle, each component wrapped in plastic.

Palmer and me, we're the first members of a new conspiracy funded by the Catholic Church to combat an ancient right-wing conspiracy disguised as a left-wing conspiracy.

This is nuts, I tell myself. It's enough to make even a John Bircher laugh.

Father John told Palmer that the entire Illuminati leadership will be meeting on Sunday night at nine. Palmer says this makes sense. They will meet so that they can be together when the power goes off, then kick back and watch the East Coast go up in flames.

Father John has the intelligence that a meeting will take place. Palmer knows where the Master he served lives. The other Princes know where the Masters they served live. All of the Princes know where the Masters like to go for their meetings.

Between all of these people, enough information is available to set up a plan.

Palmer says this meeting will give us a perfect opportunity to kill them all in one swoop, if the Princes can find and train assassins. It's a real stroke of luck.

On Sunday, my job is to kill the Grand Sovereign Master of the Illuminati as he leaves his house.

This is all my idea, and yet it's the most ludicrous idea I've ever heard.

"This is a Zeuge-78," Palmer says. "It's not government-issued. It's privately manufactured in Berlin. It's one of the best sniper rifles available."

"What does '*Zeuge*' mean?"

"It's German. It means, 'witness.'"

"Creepy."

"That's the point."

He assembles it fast, then hands it to me. It weighs about ten pounds, is almost four feet long, and looks like something out of a Tom Clancy movie.

"Here, let me fit the scope."

He snaps on a long-range scope and bipod for shooting while lying down, then threads on a suppressor at the end of the barrel for a nice, quiet shot.

"The term 'sniper' was first used during the British occupation of India in the nineteenth century," Palmer tells me. "The first sniper units were used in the American Civil War. The Germans were the first to use special-trained snipers, though, in World War I. In World War II, if a German sniper got fifty kills, the Reich gave him a wristwatch. If he got a hundred and fifty kills, he got to go on a hunting trip with Heinrich Himmler."

"Really," I say.

My basement is cold and damp and I'm shivering.

"A sniper is a one-man army, Chad. Assassins have started and won wars with a single shot. In Vietnam, it took an average of fifty thousand rounds for the grunts to get a single kill using

M16s, at a cost of twenty-three hundred dollars. For the snipers, it took an average of one-point-three rounds per kill, or a cost of twenty-seven cents."

Palmer knows a lot about stuff that most people don't want to know.

"The Zeuge-78 has a fiberglass stock with a one-inch decelerator pad and an ergonomic design. That and the bipod give you control. You have to be able to control the rifle for your first and, if necessary, your second and third shots. Next to the rifle's design, this is most important to accuracy. It's got a standard Remington trigger, retuned by German engineers. It's a good trigger, used by the Marine Corps for more than thirty years. Trigger pressure is set at two and a half pounds. You don't want to fire accidentally, so remember that. The trigger won't freeze in the rain or seize up from dirt. This here is the safety. It's got three positions, see. The cheekpiece on the stock is adjustable. You adjust it like this. This rifle is a work of art. Personally, I like the Tango-51 and the Dakota T-76 Longbow a little better, but that's a matter of personal preference. This is one of the best rifles you can get."

"Um," I say.

"Go ahead, get down there and try it out," he says, sounding like the proud father giving his son his first BB gun.

I do what I'm told, lying on the cold cement floor and resting the stock against my shoulder while Palmer starts wolfing down a sandwich.

"Good form, Chad. You're a natural. The Zeuge will give you a zero-point-five MOA at one hundred meters. That's real accurate. Even better, it's consistent and you'll get similar accuracy for your second and third shots in case you need them. It's semi-automatic, holds five rounds, and uses a popular sniping round that is good up to eight hundred meters. The ammo we'll use for the assassination is full metal jacket. It will stop anything cold."

Spooks like Palmer talk about their guns the way muscleheads talk about their Camaros. It's practically sexual.

Happiness, as the song goes, is a warm gun.

Then again, a spook's gun, if it operates properly, really is his best friend. If it doesn't, then the spook is a dead man.

Whenever there are matters of life and death, you'll find a lot of superstition and special attention to things like details.

"How do I size up the range?" I say, playing with the scope.

"The Christian Soldiers also gave us a laser rangefinder with an infrared scope for night vision. I'll show you how to use it later."

"Okay. What's in those other crates? They looked heavy as hell when those guys were carrying them."

"Sandbags. For practice."

"So is it true that Mr. Rogers was a sniper in the police or in Vietnam or whatever?"

"No. That's just an urban legend, Chad."

My good idea is becoming all too real to me.

Palmer says, "You've got a tough job. First, we have to get you to a secure location on the Master's estate with a clean shot at him when he leaves the house. Or we put you in a window at the location where he will show up for the meeting."

Holding a rifle in my hands, it doesn't seem like a very good idea at all.

"The best way to do something like this," he says, "is a classic covert-ops ambush, with two-man teams—one shooter and one spotter—setting up a triangle of crossfire to ensure the kill. That's how Kennedy was killed. Don't believe for a minute that Oswald got three accurate shots off with a cheap bolt-action Italian rifle with a bad scope in six seconds."

"I don't know if I can do this, Palmer."

He looks at me and says, "All right, Chad."

"I mean, why don't we pay some real hit men to do it? People who know what the hell they're doing and, you know, don't mind doing it."

"The Mafia and the Illuminati use a lot of the same profession-al assassins," he says. "I can't use them or it'd tip off the bad guys. If I try to get anybody else, I've got to deal with the Mafia

itself, and that would not be safe. We have to operate totally outside the box."

"Why don't we just get Father John to do it?"

Palmer snorts. "He'd love that. But I don't trust him one bit."

"This whole thing just seems silly, Palmer. It's stupid and it's
crazy."

That's what a good night's sleep, even a few hours, will do for
you. You wake up the next day and you're a normal person again.

"I thought that this is what you wanted to do. It was your idea."

With a good night's sleep, you don't think as rashly. In short,
you're no longer as brave as you were the day before. In fact,
you're scared shitless by the idea of shooting somebody in the
head at a hundred yards with a high-powered sniper rifle.

I am a lot of things, good and bad, I suppose, but I'm not a murderer or an assassin.

Plus whenever I think about this goddam conspiracy, I feel
powerless.

"We're just two guys," I say. "How can two guys fight the
Illuminati? They control the government, for chrissake."

"They don't control the government, Chad. They just influence
it. And as for two guys, or even one guy, influencing history, listen: Suppose for just a minute that Lee Harvey Oswald really was
a lone crazed gunman. Remember that President Kennedy had
threatened to dismantle the CIA and get us out of Vietnam. Then
Oswald, the crazy loner, shoots Kennedy with a magic bullet, and
Lyndon Johnson steps in, reaffirms the CIA and throws the country headfirst into war, making the military-industrial complex
hundreds of billions of dollars. American history takes this sharp
turn because of the actions of one man. It can be done."

"But Oswald didn't act alone. You said that. You told me that
even Johnson himself said in 1973 that he believed that Oswald
pulled the trigger, but didn't act alone. Even Johnson thought
there was a conspiracy."

I seem to be catching on and becoming an expert on this stuff
that most people don't want anywhere near inside their heads.

Palmer snorts and says, "He should know. Anyway, it doesn't matter. The point is that it could have happened that way, it could have been just Oswald. One man, one magic bullet, and we get a whole different country with a radically different future. That's why only half the assassinations that happen are sponsored by secret societies or the government. The other half really are just plain crazy people. It's because the power of changing the world with a single bullet is too tempting for some crazies to turn down."

One man kills President Jackson, and the next thing you know, we're not paying off the national debt anymore.

Or so the theory goes.

Me, I always pictured conspiracies to operate like the mythical Hydra—you cut off one head, and it grows back while the others still try to eat you.

Palmer tells me that the power structure is shaped like a pyramid.

And besides, he says, if you cut off all the heads of the Hydra at once, it dies.

"Listen," he says, "this is a vast conspiracy but the organization itself is not vast. Its hardcore group is only twenty-six members at full strength, with another thirteen hundred on the payroll who only know a fraction of what is going on. If you kill the Masters, especially now, because the new Princes are in training and not inducted yet, you kill the Illuminati."

The only argument I have left is that I'm too scared to kill somebody, even if it means preventing a hundred thousand people from dying.

This is that moment when the rollercoaster leaves the rail and you realize you are no longer being entertained in a controlled environment.

He says, "Chad, I've got to tell you one more thing about the Illuminati conspiracy. Something I was holding back."

Even then, for a moment, you think, this is exciting. You still think you will survive.

He says, "I don't know for sure, but it's what I think the Illuminati will do after the blackout. I was holding back from telling you because it's pretty bad."

But you start to sense the physics as the roller coaster hurtles off into empty space.

"It will be one of the most horrible things you will ever hear."

Then it isn't real-life drama anymore, the kind you feel like you're watching on TV, it's the ground rushing up to meet you.

•

Palmer says that to protect our democracy, the government did a lot of dirty things to its own people during the Cold War, in the name of national security.

For example, they experimented with germs.

•

The Germ Warfare Conspiracy: During World War Two, the Japanese Army's Unit 731, also called the Ishii Corps, performed a series of germ warfare experiments on thousands of prisoners of war, including Russians, Chinese, British and Americans, in conquered Manchuria. Prisoners were exposed to anthrax, botulism, plague and other bacteria and viruses, then dissected. At the end of the war, the United States offered Ishii and his men a deal: Give us all of your data and we'll brush your incredible war crimes under the carpet and won't put you on trial. The data ended up at Fort Detrick, where America, now in the Cold War, started its own biological warfare program. Between 1949 and 1969, the Army brewed germs and sprayed them in two hundred and thirty-nine open-air tests. Some twenty-five of these were conducted on civilian populations. In one experiment, five thousand particles per minute of the *serratia marcescen* bug was sprayed on San Francisco, from the coast inward, by a minesweeper ship. *Serratia marcescen*, found naturally in water, soil, plants and animals, was considered harmless; the Army used it because it was easy to trace and with it, they could see how a biological weapon, the "poor man's atomic bomb," could impact a major American city. *Serratia marcescen*, however, turned out to be pathogenic; some people got sick and a man died. Minneapolis was sprayed, its residents told that a "new smoke-screen" was being tested. Germs were released into the Pentagon through the ventilation system. *Bacillus subtilis* was released into the New York City subway system in 1966 to test its vulnerability to biological attack; although the germ was released in one area, it spread throughout the system. According to NIOSH, *Bacillus subtilis* can cause headaches, chest pains, breathlessness, wheezing, irritation of the eyes and skin, sweating and flu-like symptoms. In 1972, after a lawsuit, the government renounced open-air biological tests on cities. In 1985, however, the U.S. Supreme Court ruled that the Army was not liable for any injuries caused by these tests on Americans.

Between 1932 and 1972, another famous study was conducted in Tuskegee, Alabama—the Tuskegee Syphilis Study—where four hundred poor black sharecroppers infected with syphilis were told that they had "bad blood"; the Public Health Service doctors allowed the disease to ravage them, using them to conduct research on the effects of syphilis, even after a cure was discovered. In another strange case, Dr. Cornelius Rhoads of the Rockefeller Institute for Medical Investigation allegedly conducted experiments in Puerto Rico in which he infected patients with cancer, writing, "The Porto [sic] Ricans are the dirtiest, laziest, most degenerate and thievish race of men ever inhabiting this sphere. . . . I have done my best to further the process of extermination by killing off eight and transplanting cancer into several more. . . . All physicians take delight in the abuse and torture of the unfortunate subjects." The governor of the island dismissed the criminal case against him, saying that Rhoads was a "mentally ill person or a man of few scruples." Rhoads, who once wrote in a letter, "What the island needs is not public health, but a tidal wave or something to totally exterminate the population," went on to oversee the set-up of Army chemical warfare labs in Utah, Maryland and the Panama Canal Zone. Between 1962 and 1976, there was a project at Fort Detrick in which monkeys were infected with a virus that suppressed the immune system. HIV, which causes AIDS, is part of the same class of viruses. According to some conspiracy theorists, AIDS was accidentally or even intentionally released. Some say intentional release was part of the Program, an ongoing effort to exterminate blacks and gays through drugs and disease.

Some conspiracy theorists claim that the extinction of humanity is already at hand through the Gulf War Syndrome. The government denied that this syndrome was the result of exposure to biochemical weapons during the war and said that it was psychological. Conspiracy theorists point to statistics that show Gulf War vets leaving the service in droves after coming home, thousands dying and many producing deformed children. They also pointed to instances where the disease was communicable. The government, say conspiracy theorists, doesn't want to admit the fact of Gulf War Syndrome (which also prevents it from recommending or providing an effective treatment) because it was President Bush who sold the Iraqis millions of dollars in hi-tech weaponry in the first place during its war with Iran.

In many American wars, it seems, Americans sold the weapons to foreign leaders who are either Hitler or are compared to Hitler.

Then there's the 1998 story of two microbiologists arrested by the FBI on felony charges of having a biological agent meant to be used as a weapon. One of the men was a former lieutenant in the Aryan Nations, a right-wing white supremacist group. He boasted that he had cultured forty petri dishes' worth of the deadly Anthrax bug in just ten days, enough to wipe out the city of Las Vegas. He had simply read about an outbreak in his home state of Ohio, then got samples from where the cows were buried.

Some conspiracy theorists see evidence that biological warfare open-air testing on large populations is still going on today, although this is expressly forbidden by law unless informed consent is gained from the test subjects. They track criss-crossing X patterns of airplane contrails in the sky that dissipate into cirrus-like clouds, calling them "chemtrails," the result of a secret government program to both change the weather and test new biological weapons. In the wake of this phenomenon, conspiracy theorists claim that many people get sick, sometimes pointing to a gooey or cobweblike material that falls to the ground. Some have taken samples and shipped them to the director of the EPA and claimed they got no response. The illness takes the form of persistent hacking cough, fatigue, aches, anxiety, nervous tics and other symptoms, and is associated with a rising epidemic of an influenzalike illness in the United States called Adult Respiratory Distress Syndrome.

•

More of the world according to Palmer. At the rate we're going, he says, the end of the world is just around the corner.

Hearing all this, I decide that there's one thing that I definitely agree with Palmer about: Information is a virus.

There have been a lot of books and movies about epidemics of killer-viruses. Palmer says *The Stand* is still his favorite, although he loves *The Hot Zone*. Me, my favorite has always been *The Andromeda Strain*.

Palmer says that they're getting people afraid of what could happen. It's all planned.

He then tells me exactly what I don't want to hear, which is that the Illuminati have access to their own bioengineered bug and can release it on the general population anytime they want. It starts out as a common cold, then becomes the flu, and then you die, drowning in your own snot, just like in *The Stand*.

This bug does have a cure, but only the government, Army and Illuminati have access to it.

The virus is called Jehovah.

The government and the Army, unfortunately, don't know that they have it.

Officially, they don't.

If you think a blackout will cause chaos, says Palmer, imagine what a killer germ sweeping across the world will do. The world is overpopulated. People are packed together like dry kindling, waiting for a spark that will start the fire.

I don't know for sure that they'll do it, he says. But like Gaines said, they are probably following the Law of Fives. We have had four major events in the past two years, two you don't want to know about, and two you already do. They need a number five, and it is likely to be Jehovah. They have the capability, the opportunity and the motive. The end game. The end of the Game.

They will distribute it in the same white, unmarked chemtrail planes that are now being used in open-air testing in dozens of countries.

It's just a matter of switching tanks from the minorly contagious germ that causes respiratory illness to the highly contagious germ that causes death.

If they go ahead with it, one-half of the world's population will die, about three billion people, according to the Illuminati's computer analysis, anyway.

This is why Gaines left the Illuminati. It was the same with the other Princes, the so-called Servants of the Adepts. All of them left within the past few years because of Jehovah. Jehovah was too sick even for them.

In the wake of the plague will come wars, rioting, looting and lawlessness. Food distribution breaks down. Wall Street closes. Entire industries and the media go out of business. Scientists die. All of the doctors die. The CDC staff dies. Half the Army dies. While another half to three-quarters of a billion people die, all the important people, their names in the FEMA Noah's Ark Index, are safely underground.

What better way to get America, what's left of it, on its knees begging somebody to take over and supply law, order, food, protection?

On September 30, 1973, Senators Frank Church (D-Idaho) and Charles McMathias (R-Maryland), made a joint statement regarding executive orders that rendered into law powers of the Federal government during a national emergency:

"The President has the power to seize property, organize and control the means of production, seize commodities, assign military forces abroad, call reserve forces amounting to two and a half million men to duty, institute martial law, seize and control all means of transportation, regulate all private enterprise, restrict travel and in a plethora of particular ways, control the lives of all Americans. . . .

"Most [of these laws] remain a potential source of virtually unlimited power for a President should he choose to activate them. It is possible that some future President could exercise this vast authority in an attempt to place the United States under authoritarian rule.

"While the danger of a dictatorship through legal means may seem remote to us today, recent history records Hitler seizing control through the use of the emergency powers provisions contained in the laws of the Weimar Republic."

The presidents granted themselves and the Federal Emergency Management Agency, or FEMA, these powers by executive order.

By the way, he says, presidents declare national emergencies quite often.

It will be checkmate, and the Illuminati will win the Game.

Or so the theory goes.

He doesn't know if the Illuminati will really go through with it, push it that far. He doesn't mean to scare me unnecessarily. He's just making connections like the rest of us.

Overall, I think it's a pretty convincing argument to wipe them out.

# 15

We set up the sandbags and place them against the far wall of my basement after moving all the junk out of the way.

Jenny was a packrat. We never threw anything away in our house. Everything got boxed up and put in either the attic or the basement. Collectibles and nice things got put up in the attic, where it's dry. Your standard junk we put in the basement. Jenny also did all our wash down there and hung it on a clothesline.

There are boxes that hold old books and others filled with Christmas lights, ornaments, and gifts we didn't want and hadn't regifted yet. There is a trunk that contains old clothes. Under the stairs are sacks of potatoes and onions, plus cans of food and a case of Coke and two cases of beer. Old furniture sits under sheets. With Jenny gone, everything seems to be coated with dust.

Overhead, a few incandescent light bulbs light the basement pitifully. The room is filled with shadows.

Palmer pins a target on the sandbags. It's a big target with the outline of a man on it. The man appears to be waving at me.

I lie on the cold cement floor at the other end of the basement, back by my workshop, where I used to refinish the furniture that Jenny brought home from yard sales and flea markets. I size up the target with my scope, set to just twenty meters.

It's like a video game. It's actually kind of fun. I am playing secret agent.

"Let's do some practice sighting," Palmer says. "Train the gun on my head."

"Is this thing loaded?"

"No. I checked it. Click the safety off so you can practice squeezing the trigger. Now size me up."

I do as I'm told, then put my brother's face in the crosshairs. Then he's gone.

I try to find him with the scope with one eye, then find myself opening my other eye so that I can see him.

"Don't do that," he says. "You have to follow your target with the scope. Your target is not going to stand there like one of those deer you used to shoot on your hunting trips."

"This is harder than I thought."

"You watch too much TV, obviously. It's a lot harder than it looks. It took six shots to kill Kennedy, and they didn't get a really good kill shot until the President's car was practically stopped dead in the middle of the street."

I grunt, following Palmer as he walks around in front of the sandbags. As he walks to one end of the wall, I see clothes that Jenny had hung up to dry on the clothesline. My heart aches for my old life for a moment.

"Focus on me, Chad. You're zoning out."

"Okay, Jesus, I'm following you," I tell him sharply.

After a while, I get the hang of it.

I am learning to become a professional assassin.

"Later on," he says, "I'll set up the night-vision scope with the laser."

I've shot deer before, I tell myself. Deer have big black eyes and feelings and parents and kids and hearts that pump real blood, and I used to kill them for food and sport.

I've never shot a human before, however.

"And I'll show you how to find the range and adjust the scope so you get an accurate shot."

Come on, Chad, I'm thinking. If you had the chance to kill

Hitler, would you do it?

Yes, I tell myself.

Who cares if he was somebody's baby once. He started World War II and massacred millions of people. He was Satan.

Okay, then you can kill this Illuminati bastard.

Unless. . . .

Unless Palmer is full of it or worse, a nut.

I tell myself again that nuts don't predict the exact day presidents get shot.

I have already started becoming two people. Jenny would love to see this. She would say, there, you see, it can be done.

Palmer says, "When you get my forehead in your crosshairs, take a breath, hold it, and then squeeze the trigger."

One version of me totally believes Palmer and knows that the only way to stop the Illuminati is for me to do my part and kill Palmer's boss.

Palmer walks around, me following him with the scope, then stops suddenly by the clothes washing machine, offering me his profile.

I size him up, wait a moment to be sure he's still, and squeeze the trigger.

*Click.*

The other version of me is still scared shitless of, well, making a mistake. Scared that I might kill somebody and find out that it was because of a theory, not reality.

"Good," he says. "You're a natural. Now do it again, slowly."

I do as I'm told.

*Click.*

This second version of me also says that if it's real, then somebody in authority should do something about it, then I can watch the good guys triumph, like in a movie. It's funny how we all believe that dramatic events in real life should follow the same logic as a movie, or our favorite shows on TV.

"Slowly," he says.

*Click.*

All those people out there who believe in conspiracy theories, I wonder what they would do if they were in my shoes. I wonder what they would do if their faith was put to the test. It's one thing to believe in a theory, it's another to act on it to commit murder.

Palmer lights a cigarette, then waves the match. I smell sulfur.

He says, "Did you feel the pressure when you squeezed the trigger?"

I tell him that I did, and he tells me to squeeze it again about ten times.

"Do that three times a day, every day, up until the big day," he says when I'm done. "I want it to be second nature to you. And always remember, squeeze, don't pull."

"Got it."

"Now let's try live ammunition."

He comes over and shows me how to load a clip of five bullets.

This is when my brain slams on the brakes and I tell him to stop. The second version of me is screaming at me to get in the truck, pick a direction and floor it.

"What is it now, Chad?"

"I feel like I'm being railroaded, Palmer! We're going too fast."

Palmer starts to say something, then relaxes, waiting for me to get it all out.

"I don't think we've considered all of our options," I tell him. "I want to stop the Illuminati but I have to believe there is some other way to do it without me shooting somebody."

"You don't want responsibility," he says.

"Fuck you, Palmer, you know what I want."

But he's right. I want it all to go away, and I want somebody else to take care of it.

"Okay," he says. "I thought we already got through all of this, but okay, let's do it. Let's talk about our options. Come up with one and we'll discuss it."

"Well, here's an idea. We could always just go to a newspaper."

Palmer eyes me warily, then shakes his head.

I say, "It is an option. If we can get proof."

"You're a naive fool," he says. "You're still brainwashed. You think the media is the watchdog of democracy, like they taught you in civics class at North Mercer? 'What's the frequency, Kenneth?' The press, the free press, should be a distant cousin of the conspiracy theorist, but it's not."

"Aw, jeez." Here we go.

"That's right, you've earned yourself a lecture. Gore Vidal said it best when he said, 'Americans have been trained by media to go into Pavlovian giggles at the mention of conspiracy.' Think about that. The media has been influenced by people like the CIA and Big Business for years. Plus there are still a lot of full-time CIA agents in the media producing domestic propaganda and influence. In the '50s, there were about three thousand people working on global propaganda efforts. By 1978, $265 million a year was being spent on propaganda, more than the combined spending of Reuters, UPI and AP. In 1977, Copely News Service admitted that twenty-three staff members were full-time paid CIA agents. In short, Chad, the press is not our friend."

"All right," I say, on the verge of a freak out. "You're right. Even with proof, nobody would believe us. And by the time a reporter confirmed our story, if he could at all, it'd be too late."

"Yeah," says Palmer, "and we'd be dead."

"Sorry that I'm a fool, Palmer. It's just that some evil naive force has brainwashed me to think murder is wrong and not to think that every one of my country's institutions is completely corrupt."

Palmer laughs, but says, "Don't blame me, Chad."

At this moment, I realize that I'm powerless and don't have a choice.

I will have to kill Palmer's boss.

"Do we have to be alone, though?"

"Our good friends the Christian Soldiers are helping us out. We couldn't do this without them. They're giving us weapons and cash and told us about the meeting of the Masters of the Illuminati on Sunday."

"Right. They make it worse, Palmer. They give me the creeps. You were right about Father John. I don't trust him either."

"Now he gets it," Palmer says, grinning. "We're all alone, each and every one of us, and you can't trust anybody. It's the basic human condition. Living with your eyes wide open and seeing the world for what it is means being a paranoid. If you don't like it, go out and buy something to make yourself feel better. Put your head back in the sand."

"Being this paranoid is not a natural part of a normal person's life!" I shout in his face. I'm fighting the urge to break something, anything. "Look at what it's doing to me."

"I'm sorry, Chad, but it's true. You get an e-mail from a friend's address that gives your computer a virus, then automatically opens up your address book and sends the virus from you to all of your friends. You buy software for your computer that was pirated and doesn't work, even though it says Microsoft on the label just like a real disk. You plug in an electric fan with a fake UL safety label on it and your house catches on fire. You answer a fake marketing call and get tricked out of your credit card number. A guy knocks on your door saying there's been an accident and after you let him in he kills you. You pick up a hitchhiker and he also kills you. You pull over and help a driver with a broken-down car and he kills you. You punch your calling card number into a public pay phone and somebody with a pair of binoculars picks it up and sells it and your phone bill shows thousands of dollars in calls to China. You register at an Internet site and it sells your private information all over the world. Somebody bought a scanner from Radio Shack before it became illegal and he's listening to your cell phone calls. You eat at a restaurant and the waiter slides your card through a recording device in his jacket and later sells your credit card data. You answer an e-mail from your credit card company and find out later you've been suckered by some guy who uses your personal information to e-mail obscenities to everybody in your address book. Your company wants to do a drug test. Your company monitors what Internet sites you visit, taps your phone and reads your e-mails. A woman at your company accuses you of sexual harassment and gets you automatically fired. At some colleges, you have sex with a girl after she's had one beer, and it's technically rape as far as those colleges are concerned. A kid accuses you of molesting her and even after you're proven innocent, the entire town you live in shuns you. The IRS might audit you. Your wife can load a program into your computer that records everything you type into it to make sure you're not having cybersex. Somebody can steal your identity. You have oral sex without a rubber and get the clap. You have regular sex without a rubber and you get AIDS. You find out your wife is cheating on you, or maybe she's just talking about missing being single and you're left constantly wondering. You leave your kids with a baby sitter and all night you want to call home. Your baby freaks out and laughs every time it watches the Teletubbies on TV, and for some reason this bothers you, although you can't put your finger on it. You spoil your kid or hit your kid and every day you wonder if the kid is going to grow up to be a normal person. Every day the media gets you scared of terrorism or killer viruses or nuclear proliferation. Every Sunday you go to church, where a paranoid religion sells you the idea of a God who loves you but might not let you get into Heaven. You want me to go on?"

"No," I say tersely. "I get your point."

"Maybe all these things will happen, maybe none of them will. That's the essence of paranoia. And as for conspiracies, shit, the American Revolution was a conspiracy, Chad. Conspiracies are about as American as baseball and comic books. Conspiracies are so common that we should have wacko theorists making web sites that reveal 'rare coincidences that just plain happen.' Now forget about coming up with any other option, because we don't have any other option, and point your rifle at the goddam target. Get your sights on his head."

Chastened, I sigh and do as I'm told, getting the target in my scope. My crosshairs center on the head of the outlined figure drawn on the paper target. Palmer's hands gently adjust my posture so that I keep maximum control over the rifle.

"Now what do I do?" I say.

"Now you shoot!"

I take a breath, hold it and squeeze the trigger. The rifle vibrates against my shoulder, making a *puh* sound, and the target sprays confetti. I smell cordite.

For a moment, we forget about our argument and eagerly check out the result.

A small thread of smoke rises from a hole in the head of the paper man.

"Good shooting," Palmer says. "How did it feel against your shoulder?"

"Pretty good, actually. Hardly a kick."

The hunting rifles I used to use for hunting, before Jenny made me get rid of my guns, had a hell of a kick. Especially the twelve-gauge.

He nods. "The Zeuge is a fine rifle. German engineering. Now do it again, but this time, shoot the chest of the target, then wait two seconds, then shoot the head. You have to keep the target in your scope until he is on the ground and dead. If you let go of the target at any moment, you waste valuable seconds. You don't want to do that, since at that moment your own life is being measured in seconds. Now get in position."

While I size up the target, he says, "I told you all that stuff before to remind you that we live in a constant state of fear, apprehension and paranoia. Paranoia is a natural condition of man in the twenty-first century. And none of it's clear cut. I didn't even get to the background radiation of our culture. What bands are cool? What TV shows are the ones to watch? What if you say something stupid while you're drunk? On what birthday are you suddenly out of touch with the young? Do you wear the right clothes, drive the right car? Are you too different? Do you fit in? Does your lawn look good? Society is a Big Brother all in itself, Chad. We're trained to constantly worry about what other people think. It's a concentration camp of the mind. We get sucked into it, obsessively buying crap, wasting our time and energy, focusing our paranoia on the wrong things. We're drowning in information! Remember, information is a virus! Now shoot!"

I fire at the target, hold it steady in my scope despite a slight buck, then reaim and shoot again. *Puh.* I check out my results using the scope. Two perfect hits.

We both whistle at the same time.

"Excellent," he says. "You really are a friggin' natural. I'm not bullshitting you this time. You scored two great shots under stress, while I was yelling at you."

I think for a moment, then say, "Palmer, I want to tell you something. Sometimes, you scare the hell out of me. You, personally."

He ignores my comment and says, "Look at me."

He points at his head.

"Remember. This is a kill."

He points at his chest.

"This is a kill. Anything else ain't a kill. One standard assassination method, usually reserved for close-up kills, involves a tap or two to the chest and a quick follow-up tap to the head. But you should just go for the head. And don't miss. My boss is an old man, but we can't count on him having a heart attack. We need a confirmed kill. So hit the kill zone squarely, Chad. Or we're all dead. You, me, Gaines, everybody. These people play for keeps."

"You really do. Scare the hell out of me."

"You don't know what it means to be scared, Chad. You don't even know what it means to be paranoid. This is still just some weird virtual reality tour for you. You're titillated, big brother, not scared. You still think you're in some goddam movie. You think that you have a choice and if you choose to ignore it, it will all go away like some bad dream or the bogeyman under your bed. Well, guess what. There really is a bogeyman under your bed. There really is a man under your car at the mall waiting to slash your Achilles tendon with a razor. And it's not happening to somebody else, it's happening to you. This is your last wake-up call, Chad. Wake up. And if you won't, wait until the Jehovah virus comes. Then you'll know real fear. When Jehovah comes, you will know what it's like to shit your pants. When the billions die from the flu."

# 16

Years ago, when I was younger, I used to lead all my decisions and actions with my head, even if my gut pulled at me a little, telling me that what I was doing was not for the best. As a result, I did a lot of rash things.

Now that I'm older, I let my gut tell me what to do. My gut is usually right. That's where real wisdom lives. My head's job is to interpret my gut's decision and then act on it.

This is called cognitive restructuring.

It happened naturally to me over time as I got older, during the process of maturity.

Now I'm thinking with my head again. My gut keeps telling me to put my head back in the sand and ignore everything that Palmer told me. If you don't believe in ghosts, my gut likes to say, then they can't come and get you. They won't exist. Even when they make noises to get attention, you can safely ignore them and say that the creaks you hear are just the house settling on its foundation because it's old.

Palmer's gotten inside my head.

I feel more alone than I ever have in my life, worse than when our parents died and Palmer ran away. Our little assassination plot was supposed to make me feel like I'm in control, but actually makes me feel even more powerless. Without my job and because it's unsafe to leave the house, I am completely isolated.

And in my house, everything reminds me of Jenny and the fact that she betrayed me.

I watch the news on the TV and all I see are pieces that fit into a larger puzzle.

I believe everything that Palmer told me, and I don't believe it. I don't know what to believe anymore.

All I know is that I'm a total paranoid and I'm making decisions about the rest of my life based on Palmer's conspiracy worldview.

This is called cognitive restructuring.

I have become a complete nut in less than a week, the kind of person I used to laugh at from a safe distance.

You can teach people to think differently just like you can teach dogs to drool on command. It's called brainwashing. Except with people you don't need a cult to become brainwashed. You can do it to yourself. Conspiracy theories are like a drug, and once you get a good high off it, you can't stop. Only more information can satisfy you. The conspiracy must always get bigger and bigger, deeper and deeper.

If only Jenny hadn't left me, throwing me off balance, crushing me, turning me into this empty vessel needing to be filled. If only I could live in a house where every single thing didn't bring up a memory of her. If only I hadn't lost my job, tearing me away from the last thing in my life that I know as normal.

If only they weren't true, I wouldn't feel so alone.

There's more.

The President got shot. Thousands of real conspiracies have already happened in history, making this one seem plausible. Three Jesuit spooks showed up and put the fear of God into me. Palmer told me about the blackout and the possible release of Jehovah. Every generation throughout history has had kooks in positions of authority who sounded credible when they pointed the finger at secret conspiracies bent on taking over the world. Then I happened to get directly involved in the whole mess.

If only these things weren't true, I could be safely ignoring

Palmer, or laughing at him, his own insanity reinforcing rather than eating away at my own sanity.

My answering machine is infected with messages. It still has Jenny's voice on the greeting saying we're not home. Dobbs called and wants to know how I'm doing. Carl Partridge wants to know why I missed bowling night. Tim Doane, a former coworker, has an idea for a web site for the mental healthcare field and wants to get together to see if I want to go in with him. Three of Jenny's friends called and want her to call them back.

Jenny was smart. She dropped everything when she left.

I don't answer the phone when it rings, even though each time I think it might be her.

I still want her back, but another part of me doesn't want her to come home and get involved in all of this. If she knew what I was up to, it would put to rest any thought she had about leaving me.

I practice pulling the trigger as Palmer told me to do.

Click, click, click.

I practice breaking down and assembling the rifle. My record so far is ten seconds.

Palmer tells me that I will be afraid to pull the trigger, as if I don't know that already. Most people are afraid to truly change the future because the past can't be changed. We make a decision, and it lasts forever.

He says that I will pull the trigger anyway, but the internal struggle I will have at that moment will make me sabotage myself. Shooting will be more an act of catharsis, like an orgasm, than simply something I have to do, like tying my shoelaces. I'll shoot late and my aim will be sloppy.

The guy I have to kill, Palmer calls him my "target."

What I have to remember, he says, is that at the moment of truth, it's me or my target. Only one of us is going to get out alive. That means everything I do, from cleaning my gun to loading the clip to framing the man's head in my crosshairs, is a matter of life and death. At that moment, there is no audience. Nobody's looking and judging my performance. It's me, all alone, tying my shoelaces and those laces must be tied perfectly or I will die.

My only problem, he says, is that I have empathy. Therefore, I must become a robot at the time of the kill. The man in my crosshairs, at that moment, is just a target.

Just the same, I shouldn't hate him either, even though my motive for killing him is that he's a monster. Emotion has nothing to do with the actual shooting. I should be devoid of any emotion. Blank out your mind, Palmer says. Be the gun.

He tells me to remember that nothing is true and that everything is permissible. The situation we are now a part of is above common morality. The government of the United States, founded on the Judeo-Christian ethic, kills criminals sentenced to death and enemy soldiers in a war, despite God himself saying it's wrong. Animals in nature kill their own kind when they have to. Only people are afraid and they're afraid because of religion, which in turn, when you get right down to it, is just another form of mind control.

Training is the answer. Training will ensure that I move automatically when it comes time to kill, that I size up my target and shoot without thinking about it.

Training is my only friend, he says.

Palmer tells that the right training will liberate my mind so that I will become a Superman, in the Nietzschean sense—able to do anything, afraid of nothing.

Meanwhile, for me, it's a struggle to eat, shower and get dressed. I want to walk around in my bathrobe all day. I don't even feel like watching football games on the TV anymore. Every time I try to escape, I'm reminded of what I'm escaping from.

Palmer makes me eat, shower, shave and get dressed.

Discipline in all things is my friend, he says. True discipline means you know that you will die someday but lead an exemplary life anyway. Look at the Samurai.

We string up another clothesline, hang the target on it, and Palmer makes it sway and move back and forth while I practice my shooting.

*Puh. Puh.*

I can smell the cordite and hear the bullets puncture the paper target and slap against the sand bags.

Palmer keeps admiring my shots and telling me I could be a professional assassin, pulling down six figures a year, if only I didn't have my little empathy problem.

The truth is, I feel powerless most of the day until I pull that trigger. Then I feel like I'm in control again. Most of the day, I'm a victim of the gods. When I pull the trigger, I am a god.

Palmer says, "Remember that discipline is your friend. 'He who fights with monsters must take care lest he become a monster.' Frederich Nietzsche."

If I do this, I believe that I will be whole again.

My head is spinning with conspiracies. As we take breaks from practicing my shooting, Palmer fleshes out the story of the Illuminati, the mother of all conspiracy theories. Every chance he gets, he tries to convince me that everything I believe is a lie, slowly cleaning out my mind so he can put new knowledge into it.

Vulnerable, I let the theories in, thinking I can handle them, but pretty soon they take over. Cognitive restructuring. Right.

John Harrell, a militiaman, once said, "We actually fear our government more than the drug cartels and the Mafia."

I want to know what these words mean. I want to understand the power behind them.

In 1990, nearly one-third of blacks living in New York City believed that AIDS was deliberately released on them by whites. Sixty percent believed the government deliberately fed drugs into black communities. Bill Cosby is reported to have said that AIDS was "started by human beings to get after certain people they don't like."

Even today, more than half of all Americans believe that a conspiracy was involved in the assassination of John F. Kennedy.

I want the Lord to come back so that he can separate the wheat from the chaff.

A bumper sticker in the 1970s proclaimed, Humpty Dumpty was pushed!

•

Looking outside my window, I see people walking on the sidewalk, living normal lives, and I envy and feel sorry for them at the same time. But mostly, I feel disconnected and raw. It feels warm and safe inside my house, but I miss my old life.

It's funny, but all I can remember now are the good things about her.

We got married barefoot on the beach in Ocean City, our friends and family gathered around us on a beautiful day. I knew I was getting married young but that's what people do in Riverdale. She was so beautiful, so perfect, that I couldn't let her go.

Jenny was beautiful the morning she kissed me goodbye for work, the day she left me. She has a naturally thin body type, and she changed her hairstyle often, which added variety, and believe me after ten years of being with the same person you need that.

She was a great cook, which explains the slight gut I've grown since I turned thirty. In the early years of marriage, men want women who are enthusiastic in bed, but later on they realize how important it is that she knows how to cook a good meal.

She packed my lunches.

She kissed me goodbye for work every day.

Remembering these things doesn't feel good. It stings.

There's more, ten years' worth of good things, little and big, that I took for granted.

The truth is, Jenny completed me, and when she left, she took half of me with her, leaving a big empty space.

That's probably my major problem in general. When my parents died, I became permanently incomplete, always craving independence, yet deathly afraid of it.

Palmer moved in fast to fill in that other half.

The Moongate Conspiracy: Some UFO buffs and conspiracy

theorists believe that NASA not only faked the Apollo Moon landing a la *Capricorn One* as well as stumbling upon extraterrestrial activity on the Moon, but are also covering up the discovery of a giant face carved into the rocky suffice of Mars by—

This is when I beg Palmer to stop.

Palmer wants to tell me about the pyramids on Mars and the serpent kings.

I don't want to hear it.

I don't want to know.

My heart is pounding.

My brain is saturated with titillation, leaving me raw, my brain somehow starving.

Starving for something.

Human contact.

A normal day. Bowling with Carl and Keith. Seeing the regulars at the corner bar. Trivial things that feel like they matter.

Jenny.

Time flows from one day to the next in a blur, trapped in a theory.

•

At night, I can't sleep. Every night of every day that brings me closer to taking a man's life because of my belief in a conspiracy theory, I fall asleep later and later.

In just two days the power will go out, or so the theory goes.

I can't sleep, and I'm lying here thinking I would gladly kill the Illuminati son-of-a-bitch, wearing a smile on my face, if I could just do it right now.

The waiting is the worst part.

Insomnia. Just the word makes you miserable. About sixty million people just in the United States go through it every year.

Here's how you fall asleep: A chemical called adenosine gradually builds up during the day, causing drowsiness. Neurons in the bottom of the brain turn off the signals that keep you awake. Then you fall asleep. If you fall asleep within five minutes, that may indicate that you're sleep deprived.

If you don't fall asleep after a long time, then you may have insomnia.

I'm lying here thinking, I'm a thirty-four-year-old unemployed mental health orderly and my brother is Cigarette Man.

According to the National Highway Traffic Safety Administration, there are more than a hundred thousand accidents each year because of driver fatigue. Sleep is necessary for the nervous system to work properly. If you get too little sleep, it's hard to do stuff like manual labor and math and remembering things. With too much sleep deprivation, you can hallucinate and experience weird mood swings and get paranoid.

Palmer says that sleep deprivation is a key technique of CIA interrogation. It's in their manual. Physical violence and even shouting is actually frowned upon, because the subject will likely become resentful and resistant, having something real to fight against. You have to break down your opponent subtly. You have to wear him out and change his mind, so to speak. This is how hostages fall in love with their captors, the so-called Helsinki Syndrome.

I believe him.

I'm lying here thinking, is paranoia caused by belief in conspiracy theories really paranoia when those theories are true?

During sleep, after a while you go into REM sleep, where you dream. During this time, your body builds up proteins, which helps memory. During this phase of your sleep, your arms and legs go through a temporary paralysis. This is so that you don't act out your dream—you know, like getting out of bed and running into a wall.

Lately, I've been having weird dreams that I'm being watched, or I'm alone in the house and there's an assassin somewhere here with me, and all he has to do is touch me with gooey poisonous fingers and I'm dead. In another dream, Jenny called me and told me she's dying, bleeding in some cold cornfield, can I come and help her.

In other dreams, I'm suffocating.

In other dreams, I'm just falling.

I wake up completely freaked out and sweating and gulping air.

I'm lying here thinking, conspiracy is a way of life, and now so are conspiracy theories. A Memphis jury declared that the Martin Luther King, Jr. assassination was not the act of a lone gunman, but of a conspiracy, in a 1999 trial. Hillary Rodham Clinton, who was first lady to President Clinton in the '90s, said there was a vast right-wing conspiracy to defame her husband. Princess Diana dies, and it must be a conspiracy, and so on and so forth.

Palmer says this is a good thing. He says the truth will set you free, which is some old quote. Pretty soon, Palmer says, it might end up becoming common knowledge that even Abe Lincoln was killed by a conspiracy, that four people were hanged for the crime. John Wilkes Booth did not act alone.

I'm lying here thinking, if you believe that coincidences are connections, then you are a conspiracy theorist. You are also automatically considered a wacko by society.

When you're isolated, you gradually push the mundane world back, and if you're obsessed with something, that something fills all the empty spaces. It starts to become your life. Adrenaline addicts need a constant supply of fresh meat.

When you don't sleep, say, if you stay up all night, your body starts overproducing adrenaline and you get a little endorphin or adrenaline high. For a brief period of time, before you become totally miserable, you are the Buddha.

They say people turn to conspiracy theories to avoid the fact that the world is a chaotic place and shit happens for no good reason.

Me, I'd like nothing better than to let shit just happen. That's my personality type.

I didn't choose this, I tell myself. This conspiracy stuff chose me.

I'm lying here, wondering if that's really true.

Outside my window, the sky is starting to pale.

I know that it's cold outside, getting colder every day. Inside the house, it's warm and toasty. Safe.

Palmer is still telling me that all this is good for me. He says I'm well on my way to living in a world that is certainly scary, but at least it's authentic.

I wake up suffocating, realizing that tomorrow, as they say, is the moment of truth.

# 17

Palmer hands me a piece of paper. It's a printout of a message from a web site bulletin board. It reads:

*New evidence that Princess Diana was slain in an assassination will come to light tomorrow! British MI-6 at the behest of the Queen of England operated in tandem with the American CIA to produce an Operation Clydesdale-type assassination (for years, MI-6 and the CIA worked together to murder a long list of European low-lifes and petty drug dealers with rigged car crashes). They were threatened by her love affair. We love you Diana and miss you. At night we can hear your celestial voice in our dreams. The smell of flowers. Time will avenge you and all the forces of light. Ordo ab chaos! —Hermes Tresmegistus*

I read it, read it again, and hand it back to him.

"Don't tell me Princess Diana is part of this, too."

Palmer grins. "I just downloaded this off of a conspiracy theory bulletin board."

I shrug at him, not knowing what he's talking about.

I'm so tired today that I don't have the energy to care. I'm uncomfortably numb. Palmer could tell me that the entire country of China was in on the conspiracy—were all going to jump at the same time to shudder the earth off its axis, and I wouldn't care.

"Here, take a look at this while you're at it, Chad."

He shows me an e-mail message that he also printed out.

*Dear Friend: This chain letter has gone around the world five times. It started in Salem, Massachusetts on May 1, 2003. Pass it on to twenty friends and family members right now. If you pass on this lucky chain letter, you will gain peace of mind and then within ten days something good will happen to you it's true. A man in Raleigh, North Carolina found a winning lottery ticket on the street after passing on this lucky chain letter and received $500. Do not break the chain. If you do not pass on this lucky chain letter to twenty friends and family members right now, bad luck will come your way. A woman in Syracuse, NY fell down and broke her hip for not sending on this chain letter, but then saw the mistake she made, sent it and got a big insurance settlement and she's happy now. A man in Eugene, Oregon did not pass on this lucky chain letter and then found out his wife was cheating on him. He wanted to kill himself. He went on-line and saw that he did not pass on his lucky chain letter. He went to a chat room and sent the letter to twenty people. One of them wrote back and this woman became his future wife. Happiness can be yours send this lucky chain letter to twenty people right now even if you are not superstitious.*

"I hate these things," I say, handing it back to him. "Talk about making you paranoid. The last one I got had a virus attached to it that crashed my computer. But I still don't get what this has to do with the Illuminati."

"These were written for us, Chad," Palmer says, grinning. "That post wasn't really about Princess Diana and this here isn't really a chain letter. They're a cover for secret messages embedded in them. You can't understand it because it's in code. Or rather, you need a cipher just to be able to read the code, then the code must be translated."

"Why do you have to put everything in code? Don't tell me the Illuminati are monitoring the entire Internet."

"Actually, they are, sort of. They have access to the world's largest intelligence-gathering network—Echelon. Don't look at me like that—if you read the foreign press instead of our own censored press you would know about it. It's a spy network of American, British, Canadian, Kiwi and Australian agents gathering intelligence from ships, radar and communication intercept sites, planes and satellites that ring the earth. In the old days, it was used to keep watch over the Soviets. Today it's mostly used for espionage against terrorists in Europe and America. The Americans gather intelligence on the British and give it to MI-6, and the Brits gather intelligence on Americans and hand it over to the CIA. The Europeans have been in an uproar about it for years, accusing the Americans of economic espionage. A Canadian agent accused his own government of doing the same to undercut American bids on big foreign contracts. You probably never heard of it because our own press has been mysteriously silent about it. Anyway, the Illuminati can tap into this network and they can read e-mails."

"You sound so sure of yourself that I almost believe you," I say.

Palmer smiles.

"So who's the message from and what's it say? Good news?"

"Dr. Gaines posted the bulletin board message and sent me the e-mail. That's his code name in the Illuminati: Hermes Tresmegistus."

"What's yours?"

"Simon Magus. Listen, this is fantastic news. Dr. Gaines said that the other Princes are ready with their own assassins. Really fantastic. We might just pull this off yet! Gaines recruited an inmate who was discharged at the same time he was."

"Gaines is out of County?"

"Yeah," says Palmer. "As soon as we left, he walked out. Don't ask me how."

"I don't care. Okay, he's out. Whatever."

I don't work there anymore, so it shouldn't matter do me what they do with the patients.

"In the other postings, I found out that most of the other Princes recruited hardcore conspiracy theorist aficionados and five of them actually recruited militia. That was smart of them. The militia have military training."

"Those people are freaks."

At the same time, I'm thinking, so there are people who believe in this stuff enough to kill for it, not just the occasional nuts like Timothy McVeigh.

"Freaks? They're your only hope to fight the Illuminati government that's coming. Too bad that most of them will die of Jehovah, and the rest will be recruited into the government's paramilitary police once the dictatorship is born. Today's anti-government militia will be tomorrow's National Defense Force, tomorrow's stormtroopers."

"So every single point of opposition to dictatorship is actually going to become an asset of the dictatorship," I say, admiring the sick beauty of it.

Palmer nods. "That's pretty much right. They've thought of everything."

"Nothing surprises me anymore. Anything you say. The Boy Scouts are going to tell on their parents and have them put in concentration camps. Fine."

My mind is on more practical matters. What I want to know, I tell him, is if the other assassins are ready to do their job. After all, tomorrow we have to kill thirteen men in a perfectly coordinated attack. And if we fail, the Vatican and the Illuminati will be after us.

Palmer is still nodding. "They've been training for days, just like us. That was the posting. The e-mail confirms that they're ready. It's a thumbs-up in code."

•

Sitting at my kitchen table, Palmer draws me a map of the

estate of the Grand Sovereign Master of the Illuminati, the one guy in the world who has more power than the President of the United States. Tomorrow is the big day, and my stomach won't stop doing backflips. Tomorrow, this will all be over.

I get the grand prize, Palmer says. The top of the pyramid. The Grand Master himself. The boss.

The kitchen is nice and toasty, heated by a wood-burning stove.

Outside, the sky is overcast and it's a cold, damp, miserable day.

Maybe one or two of the assassination attempts will fail, he says. One or two of the Masters might get away. They can be finished off later. But we cannot miss when it comes to the Grand Sovereign Master. He must die or we're dead.

"I'll get him," I say.

I get up, put the kettle with water under the kitchen faucet, and pour enough water to make some instant coffee.

"Let me explain it further," Palmer says. "If we don't kill the Grand Sovereign Master, we're really dead. He will definitely panic and order the release of Jehovah, whether the Illuminati were planning to or not."

When Palmer says we're dead, he means we're all dead.

I turn on the gas stove and put the kettle on the orangish-blue flame.

"Oh," I say.

Nothing like a little extra pressure to help you with your first assassination attempt.

"This is the Master's estate. Most of it is built on the principle of the Golden Section."

"Brother, you've lost me already."

"The Golden Section is a rectangle with a ratio of five to three used by the ancient Greeks to build the Parthenon and many other buildings. Fibonacci of Pisa expressed it as a number, 0.618034. It is a number found in architecture and art and music. Its spirals are also everywhere in nature, from snail shells and pinecones to sunflower heads and galaxies. Kepler called it one of the two treasures of geometry. It has been called the Divine Proportion or the Golden Ratio. It has great mystical significance."

I stare at Palmer for a moment, then say, "So everything here on this map is rectangular, is what you're saying."

"Yes."

He shows me how to get onto the grounds without being detected by the surveillance cameras, then he points out a spot in some shrubs from which I'll have a clean shot at the front door.

When the Grand Sovereign Master of the Illuminati, a man in his sixties wearing a dark suit, comes out the front door to go into his limo, I'm supposed to shoot him down. I will be just seventy-five yards from my target.

Palmer says that the limo will pull up in the driveway and park about fifty feet from the front door of the house, leaving its motor running. The average human walks four miles per hour, so that means I will have about seven seconds to score my hit, about the same amount of time it allegedly took Oswald to hit Kennedy three times with a cheap rifle.

The Master will be protected by a small army of the notorious men in black, so shoot, confirm the kill, and run like hell.

"You have to shoot from an angle," he says. "You don't want that car between you and the target. Just lie on the ground starting at six and keep your sights on the door until he comes out. He'll probably come out between six and six-thirty. It's going to be cold out there waiting. Do you have thermal underwear?"

"Where is he, Palmer? I mean, where am I going to do this?"

Palmer considers for a moment. He's still holding back information about the Master, keeping me on a need-to-know basis, I assume, for my own protection—why or exactly against what, I'm not sure.

"What's the big deal? I'm going to have to know who he is if I'm going to do this."

"The big deal is that Father John's coming over tomorrow with his Christian Soldiers, just before you head out to kill the Grand Sovereign Master, and he's going to do an inspection."

"We're on the same side though, right?"

"Right, but if he doesn't like what he sees he might decide to kill us."

I'm shaking my head in disbelief.

"Every secret society has its rituals about killing its enemies," he says. "The ancient Greek followers of Bacchus used to tie you up in a cavern and send you down a slide into the bowels of the earth, to be carried off by the gods if you were lucky, or starve to death if you weren't. The Illuminati flay star-shaped patches of flesh off of you before disemboweling you. Consider Jack the Ripper: He was an Illuminati Prince who went off his rocker. The Christian Soldiers usually just put a bullet through your head or strangle you, then feed you to pigs."

"Sick fuckers," I say, resisting an urge to spit. "All of you. So he might kill us or not kill us depending on whether we kiss his ass or not. I still don't get why. It's all about power, isn't it. Who has the biggest shlong. They'll kill us just because they can."

"No, it's quite practical," Palmer tells me. "If we don't look like we know what we're doing, then Father John will believe that we'll botch the assassinations. If the assassinations get botched, then the Illuminati will realize their vulnerability and go even deeper into secrecy, making the Christian Soldiers' job that much harder. They'll have to kill us."

The kettle starts to whistle, and I get up and fix us two hot mugs of coffee.

"Lots of milk and sugar in mine," Palmer reminds me.

"Right."

He rubs his hands in anticipation. "Coffee, coffee, coffee."

I set his mug before him.

He says, "Before they kill us, they'll torture us to find out if we know anything about the Grand Sovereign Master so maybe they can try their own assassination or just conduct surveillance. This is a practical business. There's no morality but there's no sadism either."

"All right," I tell him. "I figure I don't want to know."

I drink my coffee.

"Princeton," he says.

"Christ, Palmer. I thought you weren't supposed to tell me."

"I won't tell you his name yet. I can tell you where he lives. He lives in Princeton."

The Master of the World lives in Princeton, New Jersey, a half-hour from where I live.

He says, "You'll see some guys come out of the house first and do a sweep of the car for bugs and bombs. Then they'll give a signal and the Master will come out. At that moment, you can see them but they can't see you. They're sitting ducks. You'll feel like God."

"Is that what you called him, Jesus? 'Master'?"

Palmer gives me a sharp look. "Let's stay focused here, Chad."

Sometimes my disgust for all this gets the better of me.

"Is that all, then?"

"No," he says. "I have to get you on the property and navigate you past the security cameras to the exact spot. This is way harder than it sounds. You'll be dressed in black to help avoid detection. You're going to have an earpiece and a mouthpiece so I can communicate with you. You'll have a transmitter on you and I'll be able to track your exact position with a laptop linked to the global positioning satellite network."

All I have to do is what Palmer tells me, then shoot when the Master appears.

"There's another tricky part," he says. "When you shoot the Master, his people may decide to cut off the power anyway. Don't be surprised if that happens. But at the very least we'll be able to save several billion people dying of plague and a worldwide totalitarian police state."

I look out the window and see the people passing on the sidewalk that borders the yard. I don't recognize any of them. This time, one of them turns, looks at the house, and laughs soundlessly. He's just laughing at some private joke he remembered, but for a second I could swear that he's laughing at me.

This makes me even angrier at the world.

Palmer gulps down the rest of his coffee and says, "You need to lighten up, Chad."

I glare at him, wondering why I still don't know my own brother.

I talk to him, and it's like talking to a conspiracy textbook. There's no person behind the network of theories and blizzard of information.

Why didn't he cry at our parents' funeral?

Why did he suddenly become social at school after they died?

Why did he become the perfect student, painstakingly make lots of friends, take a girl to the prom and so on, when I could tell, seeing him at home, that he hadn't really changed?

Knowing Palmer back then meant knowing a mask, and that's true today.

He's truly creepy, an enigma, and if he weren't my brother, I would definitely not be trusting him right now even if I believed him.

I won't pull the trigger until I find out, though. He's going to tell me everything. It's my going rate for murder. To know my brother. To know why he didn't cry.

Palmer says, "We're having company tonight. Friends of ours. We'll have a little party. It should take your mind off everything and help you sleep and forget everything about the past that's still bothering you. You need it. Remember, tomorrow's the big day."

# 18

Industrial music is blasting from my stereo, people are laughing and talking, and I'm staring at everything with fascination, exploring an alternate state of consciousness thanks to the drug that Palmer slipped into my drink.

"If you want to live, dial 911," he says.

My living room is filled with Illuminati Princes and conspiracy theorists, drinking and laughing like the humans and the pigs at the end of *Animal Farm*. In this Game in which people die and nations and markets are wrecked, friends are enemies and enemies are friends. Your agents run the opposition while your own controller is an enemy agent.

Somebody is writing on a wall with red lipstick:

*Check for your wallet*

I'm thinking, good and evil all come from God. The same God who kills you with cancer is the same God who will accept you into Paradise.

The drug is kicking my brain to a higher level, to the metaphysical. I'm not sure, but I'm becoming increasingly convinced that I exist. I'm on the verge of something truly original and profound that I know I won't remember the next morning when I'm sober.

The man is writing:

*It's eleven-thirty. Do you know where your children are?*

"Charles Manson got his acid from Timothy Leary," says one man that I'm pretty sure is a militiaman, judging from his beard and scar on his cheek.

"Do you think Timothy Leary, while working for the FBI, was trying to turn on Manson so that he'd trigger the black-white race war?" asks another man that I'm pretty sure is a Prince in camouflage pants. "He did write that personality test for the CIA."

It all just turns to a soup in my head, salted with babble.

"Charlie Thrush."

"Lexington Narcotics Hospital."

"Jonestown massacre."

"John Lennon knew."

"Gulf War Syndrome."

"Capitol Hill Coup—if it weren't for Smedley, FDR would have been overthrown and we'd all be Nazis."

"Ordo Templi Orientis."

"Propaganda Due Lodge."

It's like hearing another language spoken fluently by foreigners.

FBI CIA NASA FEMA GWEN HAARP CDC ATF WHO WTO DEA!

Alphabet soup.

The man is writing:

*People are talking behind my back*

Kevin is sitting on the couch like a small mountain. Kevin the psychotic whale. This is not a hallucination. He is Gaines' familiar, his minion, his assassin.

"You shouldn't drink while you're on medication," I tell him.

He stares at me, then gets up and goes into the kitchen.

"There's only love, Kevin," I call after him. "The gas chambers are all in your mind. The real world just is, and the people in it, all they want is to exist and be loved."

Dr. Gaines' bearded, smiling face is floating in my vision.

"You're a genius, Mr. Carver," he says, gesturing with his drink. "A genius!"

"I always hated your glasses," I tell him. "And you smoke too much."

He laughs loudly.

"To destroy the Illuminati once and for all—what a brilliant idea you've concocted! You make me feel like I'm in the Game again. You are truly the man of the hour and my hat's off to you. You, Mr. Carver, will never make the history books, but tomorrow you will make history. I am proud to know you."

The man is writing:

*I heard a noise downstairs*

"You should thank Palmer," I say. "He made me what I am today."

The living room expands to about twice its size. The light keeps playing tricks on me.

"No thanks," a female voice behind me says. "That shit makes me paranoid."

There are beautiful women here, and I'm pretty sure they're not a hallucination either. I'm talking *Penthouse* Pet, *Playboy* Playmate, supermodel beautiful. Blondes, brunettes, redheads in bright party dresses, sipping pink drinks and popping pills into their mouths.

I ask Palmer if they're real and he warns me not to accept any apples from them.

"Never get high on life, Chad. It's a dangerous hallucinogen."

"Is this what it means to be illuminated?"

"You're close. The whole thing, everything, is getting you close. And if you can manage to get laid tonight, then you might just hit it on the head."

"I'm married, Palmer."

"That's your construction and I respect it, even if I don't understand or like it."

"Thanks."

"Me, I've got my eye on what I want and I'm going to get it."

This is when a tall, knockout redhead approaches me, and my heart starts pounding. Redheads are either ugly or beautiful to me, but this one is beyond beautiful. She's perfect. Her skin is flawless and pale, and her eyes blaze a manic green. She's skinny and has a big chest and looks no more than twenty-one, twenty-two years old.

She looks like the type of woman who would give her man creative and energetic sex, keep him addicted to it, and put his psyche through the shredder the whole time.

After ten years of a marriage that ended with all the hideous beauty of a plane crash, a nutty gorgeous man-eater is just what I need.

"I can read minds," she tells me.

"What am I thinking right now?"

She closes her eyes and says, "You're wondering if I'm a C or a D cup. You're also wondering what it'd be like to fuck me hard."

God, just listening to her talk is getting me aroused.

The man is writing:

*Did you hear a click?*

"That's amazing," I say. "How do you do it?"

She smiles a cannibal smile. "I always know what men are thinking."

Grinning stupidly, I do what every guy does when he can't think of something to say: He repeats what the woman says as a question.

"You do?"

"Yes."

I wonder if this prostitute can now read the thoughts of Jenny that are hitting me like a cold shower, breaking through the layers of the drug so that I achieve clarity for a moment.

"So how do you know Palmer?"

The devil-woman shakes her head slowly, recasting her spell.

She leans forward while my heart rings like an alarm bell in my chest, and whispers in my ear: *Tantra*.

Tantra?

Sex magick, she says.

The woman takes me by the hand and leads me upstairs.

The man is writing:

*Do you know where she's been?*

Sex magick.

She's right about that. It's perfect, magical, like a dream. Thanks to the drug I stay detached enough not to fall hopelessly in love with her. And after several hours, I forget all about Jenny and her cheating on me, I forget about the Illuminati and the job I have to do tomorrow. I shed the past like dead skin. Nothing matters. I fall asleep, past the nightmares, and deep into a blissful oblivion.

# 19

Palmer and I are standing in the wreckage of my living room and we're smiling, sharing secrets without talking, you know, bonding. It's late in the day; I slept until four in the afternoon and woke up feeling fantastic.

"So," he says, "how was she?"

"Fantastic," I tell him. "More than fantastic. Like a dream. My dream devil-woman."

"What about your wife? How are you feeling about her leaving you now?"

"I feel better. Thanks, Palmer."

Then it slowly dawns on me that today is the day I have to kill the Grand Sovereign Master of the Illuminati at his home.

"I know what you're thinking," he says, "but before that, we have to get past Father John. If we survive that, then killing Galt will seem like a cakewalk. Trust me."

"Trust you," I say mechanically.

"I hope you're ready now," he tells me. "He'll be here any minute."

I must be turning white as a ghost, because Palmer is laughing at me.

There is a knock at the door, making me jump.

"Showtime," he says.

It's time to be judged.

Palmer answers the door and Father John steps into the house, trailed by his Christian Soldiers, his eyes smiling.

"*Buono pomeriggio, Sig. Carvers. L'oggi e un giorno grande per le forze di Christ.*"

I'd like to say something back but I can't talk. My tongue is stuck to the roof of my mouth. I can barely breathe.

"Looks like you've been festive the past few days," says Father John, surveying the ruins of the party. "But I trust you're sharp and ready to perform the task at hand."

I nod numbly, staring at the old Jesuit while he takes his coat off. Irenaeus and Hippolytus keep theirs on, standing behind him with their hands clenched at their sides.

Everybody's excited; it fills the room.

The wind blows some dead leaves into the foyer, rustling along the carpet.

Through the open doorway I can see that it's already getting dark.

"Make yourself comfortable, *Vater*," Palmer says, shutting the door against the cold. "Excuse the mess. Last night we enjoyed our last supper."

•

Down in the basement, Father John is watching me shoot the target that Palmer set up.

"Bravo," he says. "You're a natural, Mr. Carvers."

"Thank you, Father," I tell him, peering into the scope.

"He just woke up," Palmer says, smiling. "And he can still hit the target."

Palmer is taking it easy on me. He's not swinging the target around too much. We've practiced under much more difficult conditions. Still, it's hard to hit the target with so much pressure. What's more pressure, I wonder, shooting knowing you will kill a man, or shooting knowing that a man might kill you?

Training. Discipline. My rifle. These are my friends.

I blank out my mind and shoot, hit the target.

Then Palmer throws me a curve ball, swinging the target erratically, even wilder than we'd ever practiced.

I miss. The bullet smacks into the sand bags.

Without thinking, I immediately pull the bolt, shoot again and hit the target.

Training. Discipline.

"*Maravilloso*," says Father John, then tells me, "If the Illuminato weren't to be destroyed tonight, I would try to recruit you."

"That's quite a compliment, Chad," Palmer says.

I reload the rifle and wait for the next test.

"Mr. Carvers."

"Yeah, Father?"

"Tonight we will celebrate the victory of the forces of Christ."

"Yeah."

I'm nodding and thinking, just keep nodding.

"The forces of light will triumph over Satan, and Satan will be returned to the pit. Then all the world will know right and wrong. All the world will take a step closer to God."

"I guess so," I say, confused. "I mean, sure."

"*Bueno*. Irenaeus, Hippolytus and I will stay here and pray for your success and that of your comrades at arms."

Just then, Father John stares me hard in the eyes and I can feel myself breaking. In a moment, he knows that I know something and that I will crack under torture in less than ten seconds. He smiles, but his eyes are distracted, as if he's weighing a hard decision.

In the Game, what people say does not matter. You have to watch what they do. Even then, you have to interpret.

At last, his smile broadens, becomes more genuine, less deadly.

"We are satisfied," he says. "We have made a wise investment. God bless you, my son."

"Thanks," I manage to say after some stammering.

We made it. We passed the test. He's not going to kill us.

"Excellent, *Vater*," Palmer says, then blows Father John's head against the wall.

•

My ears are ringing with the explosion and in the flash of smoke and powder my mind replays the event: Palmer reaching up with my handgun, holding it an inch away from Father John's smiling profile, and pulling the trigger.

The Jesuit's smile dissolved as his head exploded and his blood and brains sprayed against the far wall.

The Swiss drops to one knee while lifting a pistol fitted with a silencer.

Palmer's second and third shots burst smoking holes in his chest, and with a groan Irenaeus crumples backward, falling painfully on his own legs, until he lies on his back with his pelvis in the air. The pistol falls to the ground, still gripped in the man's hand.

Palmer walks up to the body and fires two more shots into him, one in the chest and the second in the face. Blood splashes outward in a wide semi circle on the floor around the man's head, forming a halo of red splatter.

The echoes of the shots make my teeth hurt.

I turn, almost too late, to see Hippolytus advancing on me in his black coat, holding a cord in his bare fists.

"Please don't," I tell him, but I'm frozen, holding the rifle pointed at his chest.

He looks into my eyes and smells my fear.

"Don't," I tell him again, my voice as high as a woman's, almost a shriek. "Stop."

He continues his advance, coming at me nice and slow, his eyes locked on mine.

"Get away from me."

His expression doesn't change. The Sicilian doesn't appear to be panicked or even angry at what Palmer's done to his comrades. Instead, he seems to be drawing strength from me, growing more powerful and invincible while I grow weaker.

In another moment, I know that I will drop the rifle and let him kill me.

I close my eyes and fire.

*Puh*

I hear a ripping sound and open my eyes. Hippolytus is staggering backward, his face a mask of pain, a puff of smoke rising from a hole in his coat. Suddenly, I see fear in his eyes, the fear of death, and I feel all of his strength flowing into me. I am a god now. Fuck you, I think. Fuck all of you. I fire again, blink at the crack of the ricochet, and see Hippolytus holding his throat, blood rushing between his fingers.

I just want him dead. I don't want him to suffer. I just want him to die. This man told me once that he was sorry that my wife left me. Now his lips are moving, rapidly, without sound. I walk up to him calmly and press the edge of the silencer against his forehead. My eyes are wide open. This is the single most horrifying moment of my life.

I pull the trigger.

The back of his head bursts.

●

I stand over the smoking corpse, on the edge of crying, throwing up and passing out.

This is not me, I tell myself. I work at a hospital. I'm married. My wife and I, we've been talking about maybe having kids and starting a family.

I take care of people at work and at home. I'm respectable, the kind of guy who gives people a hand when they need it. Everybody knows me and they trust me. I trust them back. I'm not alone. I'm not infected with conspiracy theories. I'm not paranoid and part of the Game. I didn't just kill a man in cold blood.

This can't be happening.

This is happening.

I manage to ask, "Why did this happen, Palmer?"

I remember when I was a kid and somebody twice my size

trounced me for no reason. I didn't mind the pain at the time. The humiliation was worse. But what I really wanted was to know why. I wanted to understand the evil that comes with a complete lack of empathy. To me, at that time, this was the most horrible reality in the world, and I knew fear.

Palmer shrugs, lights a cigarette, and tells me that philosophy is lived in the details.

I ask him, "Why did we do this?"

Now he's standing at my side, looking down at the lifeless form of Hippolytus.

"Nice work," he says, impressed. "You were better than I'd thought you'd be. It was a good experience for you. Like a warm-up."

I step away from him, repulsed. "You're fucking crazy, Palmer."

Palmer shrugs again, his hands freckled with drying blood, and smokes his cigarette.

He gestures with it.

"Want one?"

"Crazy fucking asshole," I tell him, full of venom, but I can't muster rage. If I could, I would be beating Palmer to a pulp right now. Instead, I'm exhausted, barely able to move.

He blows smoke in a long stream.

"This is not about right and wrong, Chad. That's your construction. Don't get all indignant on me. This solved a lot of problems we might have ended up having."

"They were on our side, I thought."

"Sure they were. We sold them good. But they couldn't be trusted. Father John was one of the Black Popes in the flesh. I'm sure of it."

My head is spinning.

There is no more creeping bullshit. I don't believe in that anymore. There is only reality.

"How can I trust you, then?"

"Expedience," Palmer says. "You know I want you to kill the

Master and save the world from a plague that will make this look like nothing, less than nothing."

Expedience is the first law of nature, he says.

The wolf knows nothing about morality. It tears out the throats of sheep and then eats them. That does not make it evil.

"We're not animals."

"Right, and that's why it's best not to have loose ends with most people. Because animals can always be trusted to do what's expedient. With man, you have to assume the worst."

He calls that the second law of nature.

These laws contradict each other, but I don't feel like debating with him about it.

"You could have told me."

"I didn't feel like debating it for ten hours. It was better this way. Necessary."

"You're a psychopath," I tell him.

"Psychopaths kill without reason. I killed these men for a reason. So did you."

"That's right. I was protecting myself."

"So was I."

"No, you weren't. They weren't going to do anything to us. We both knew it."

"Oh, so you were protecting yourself when you executed this soldier? Is that what you call it?"

"I was out of my mind, Palmer!"

"Well, if that's what it takes for you to get in touch with what you want, fine. Me, I don't need to be out of my mind to do it." He kicks the corpse harshly. "It's just meat, Chad. A dead man. But the truth remains: Nothing is forbidden. Everything is permissible."

It's when you actually kill a man that you understand these words in their fullness. I know that understanding these words can make you free, but also more alone than you've ever felt in your life. This is how psychopaths feel when they become serial killers. Like a god, a lonely god, beyond good and evil, beyond truth. To be a god, one must create or destroy. Some people paint, others write, others kill.

He hands me a black and white photo and a color photo, both taken of the same man, a man around sixty years old, stern, his eyes magnetic. Not a flabby old sixty but a distinguished hard sixty, the kind of guy you expect to see running a steel or railroad empire.

Palmer says that he kept these photos in a little file as insurance against the Illuminati knocking him off. Copies are kept in five separate safety deposit boxes at various banks.

"I thought they owned the banks," I tell him viciously.

"He wears glasses," Palmer says. "Little round glasses. Remember that."

I know who this man is.

No horns, tail or pitchfork. Just a sixty-year-old guy.

Just one man who has many names.

Majestic Wizard of the Ages, High Priest of the Anointed Adepts, Commander of the Four Elements, Lord High Seer of the Ancients, Illuminatus Augustus, the Puppet Master himself, the Master of the World. . . .

Grand Sovereign Master of the Order of Perfectibilists.

"Emmet Galt," says Palmer.

"Emmet Galt," I say, holding the photos.

"Spartacus."

"Spartacus?"

"That's his code name in the Illuminati. Every Grand Sovereign Master is Spartacus and has been for nearly two thousand years. If I had been able to take his place, it would have become my name, and I would recruit a new Simon Magus to take my place."

Spartacus.

"Learn that face well. The next time you see it, it'll be in your crosshairs."

I stare at the face in a state of mild shock, struggling to make the final connection between a giant shadowy conspiracy and a single man made of flesh of blood.

Palmer says, "Kill this man and you will save the world."

I look at my brother, trying to read him, but it's like reading a book about conspiracy theories, one that shows you everything but tells you nothing.

Palmer smiles a smile that could only be described as evil.

"Yes, you're right, I'm a bastard, Chad. To you, I'm a snake. I know that. And that makes you suspicious of me. I'm the perfect villain to you. You've been trained by your religion to hate me, by movies, by your society. I'm a monster, fine. Guys like me are always double-crossing the good guys at the end, that's what you think, which is another indication that you've been asleep your whole life and live in a fantasy world. Well, wake up, because this isn't a movie. This world you're in, with me, is authentic. There are no good guys and bad guys, only people who want what they want. Some are willing to do only certain things to get it, other people are willing to do anything. When I kill, it is for expedience, not joy. Sometimes, it's simply necessary. That's the only expectation you should have of me, that I do what I must, nothing more, nothing less. Now consider this: I am the only one who can get you where Galt will be in less than an hour, and if you don't get to him, Galt will likely wipe out most of the human race. I am not fucking kidding. When the real God comes to wipe out the whole earth with fire as he promised, it will be Lucifer who tries to stop him. Well, there it is, Chad. You can walk away right now and forget about it and let most of the world die and the Illuminati win, or you can make a deal with the devil. There is no good and there is no evil, only what you want and how you're going to get it. So what's it going to be?"

●

It's dark and I'm driving to Emmet Galt's house like a good soldier.

My truck rattles and it's drafty inside, filling the truck with the smell of combustion, gas and oil burning to create force to turn the wheels. I have always liked that smell. It's a good clean honest smell, good like the smell of hot coffee steaming into cold air, and it reminds me of long drives home.

Usually, when I'm not driving with Jenny or a buddy of mine, the radio keeps me company. I click it on but the music sounds like noise. I click it off.

My mouth is dry and I'm trembling. I turn up the heat, and it blasts dry against my hands and chest until I sweat under my clothes.

Beneath me, under the seat, is a case that holds a Zeuge sniper rifle.

I'm not actually going to kill Galt. I'm going to detach and watch myself kill him from a safe distance.

I have to think this way, because the oncoming headlights glaring through my windshield look attractive to me right now, drawing me like a moth, and I have the urge to jump.

Palmer says in my ear, *How are you reading me now, Chad?*

"Fine," I say, hating the idea of conversation. I'm all business now. I just want to get there and get it over with, then figure out what I'm going to do about Palmer.

There are three dead bodies in my basement. Their blood is all over the walls.

I taste my own bile and swallow hard against the urge to throw up.

*I've got you on Route 518 heading northeast, towards Princeton.*

"Yes," I tell him, gripping the wheel, "that's exactly where I am."

*Good.*

Palmer sounds satisfied. All his little gizmos work.

I say, hey Palmer.

He asks me what I want.

What I want is to finally get inside his head. He owes me that now.

"Tell me a story."

Palmer chuckles in my ear.

This is what it's like to be a paranoid schizophrenic, I'm thinking. You hear disembodied voices.

*What kind of story do you want to hear?*

"I don't want to hear about another conspiracy. Anything but that."

All right, he says.

I say, tell me about the treefort. Tell me why you ran away and left me with nothing. Tell me why during the time after Mom and Dad died you got close to everybody at school except me. Tell me why every time I'm with you it's as if I'm with somebody I don't know.

The earpiece doesn't talk for a few minutes. I'm out in the country now, keeping an eye out for deer, and it's dark. I have my highbeams switched on. The road rushes under me and a part of my mind counts the yellow lines, pretending they're laser beams like I did when I was a kid. I'm listening to the sound of the tires on the road, the hum of the engine. I become hypnotized by that sound, feeling peaceful for the first time in days.

Palmer's voice crashes in my ear like a brick through the windshield.

*You want to hear about me, then. You want to get inside my head, don't you. Have a heart to heart like brothers. Even after all you've heard this week, even after you shoot a man, you still can't stop being sentimental. You're the guy in the movie who won't shoot in the back; you have to give the villain a chance to raise his gun and have a crack at you before you fire. The guy with the big heart. The giver. My big brother.*

"Yes, Palmer," I tell him, my voice edged with rage, "I want a brother. Even a brother who is a murderer."

*The Illuminati didn't contact me when I was sixteen. It happened much sooner.*

I stiffen, alert, waiting for more.

*When I was four years old, I thought that I was on a TV show that God watched. I could feel him watching me constantly. I thought that everyone was an actor, including you, and that when you all left the room you'd look at your lines.*

I'm listening.

*Then I stopped believing in God. Then I thought that everyone was an alien and I was being observed in some sort of experiment, maybe a zoo.*

I'm listening.

*I never believed in Santa Claus and I never really believed in God, but I had always believed in secrets—anything that was a mystery. You could say I had conspiracy in my blood. When it came time for me to grow up like other people and see the world differently by degrees, I resisted it. I stayed detached. I didn't want to give up the mystery. I instinctively knew that reality was horrible, boring, and I wanted nothing to do with it.*

He says nothing for a while. Neither do I. I know that he can hear me breathing.

*Something happened to me, Chad. I'll tell you about it. I'll tell you about it because it's important to you, like it's important to so many typical ignorant people, to know all of the shit that's inside other people's lives and heads. I'll tell you. It happened to me, and I was able to stayed detached forever. I never developed what you would call empathy. I didn't care about other people at all. They are things to me. They are things because I can't let them near me, inside my head, or I'd be vulnerable to attack. I'd also have to get involved in their meaningless lives. I'd have to give up all the mystery. This is me, Chad, your brother. Like I said before, the real me is ugly to you. The real me doesn't care much about you or anybody but myself. The real me doesn't see any other world except mine.*

"Tell me what happened," I ask him, my voice almost a whisper.

*I was walking in the woods and a man found me and said I was chosen. He said that he would raise me and that I would be privy to the most ancient of mysteries. Then he basically molested me. After that, I came to see him often in the woods. I would wait for him in the treefort. He taught me there. His name is Emmet Galt.*

Oh, I say.

In some ways, shock is a good thing. It keeps your head from reeling. Everything becomes like a dream, and you watch it from a great distance, comfortably numb.

*That's when I refused to grow up and deal with people and, for lack of a better word, reality. A few years after I was first molested, I was given a test to see what I had learned. That's when the Illuminati killed our parents. That car crash they died in, well, it was arranged.*

I say nothing. Instead, my brain is racing, trying to assimilate this information. I already knew it, somehow, and now that it's out in the open, I feel a strange relief.

Catharsis is like being reborn.

*All of this was designed to tell me that life is not a TV show with a happy ending, that even the high and mighty can become cripples and end their lives begging on the street, spit on by people. Life is pain and gives you no favors. We are all alone in the Universe, all alone except for ourselves. We can create the world, Chad, in our own minds, and it can be a fantasy or a reality. My test was to be everything that everyone wanted me to be, even though my parents were dead. I was not allowed to grieve. I was not allowed to shed a tear. Instead, I had to be perfect. I joined the wrestling team with the other hairless monkeys. I went to the junior prom with a date and had sex with a girl for the first time that night. I was in the school play. I had to be the perfect student, the perfect everything. I spent all my time around people so that I could learn to mimic them, get them to like me.*

I realize that I was right all along. Palmer is nuts.

*You're speeding up, Chad. You're going too fast. Slow down.*

Out of his mind, crazy, nuts.

*When I proved that I had tasted true freedom and could live without guilt, love or a concept of sin, Galt said that I was ready to be formally initiated into the Mysteries. Four years later, I became the youngest Prince in the Illuminati. When Hasan bin Sabah inducted new members into his Assassin cult, he had them drugged; they woke up stoned on strong hallucinogenic hash in a cool pleasure garden that was filled with beautiful willing women. After a few days, they woke up back in their normal lives, and would do anything for Sabah to get back in that garden. Sabah said, die a glorious death for me, and you will enter that Paradise again. I lived in that Paradise for ten years. It was what I gave up when I left them. And because I was going to leave them, and they knew where I was going, they wouldn't kill me, but they would try to hurt me.*

"Shut up, Palmer," I tell him, savagely.

I don't want to know.

The clues were there all along.

Father John said, "I understand, and do regret, that your wife has disappeared."

He didn't say that Jenny left me. He said that she disappeared. I knew then what had happened, but I didn't want to know. I don't want to know now.

*They killed Jenny, Chad. I'm sorry but that's what happened.*

"Shut the fuck up!"

The tears finally come.

I've finally found my catch phrase to make me cry over Jenny leaving.

Tears pour out of my eyes until I can barely see. My great big cry has finally come.

The catch phrase goes something like this: "She was innocent."

Crying in waves, blinded by it, drowning in it.

The earpiece is silent.

I step on the gas, press the pedal to the floor. The engine responds with a brief roar.

"There's more to this you're not telling me, Palmer."

*That's it, my brother. You now know the truth.*

"Nothing is true."

Palmer says nothing.

"I think you want Galt dead for another reason. Is it because he molested you?"

*He's going to kill most of the world's population, Chad. I told you.*

"That's a theory, you murdering sack of shit."

*He's at least going to turn off the power. That will definitely happen. And as for the rest, well, go ahead. Roll the dice and see what happens. See what happens when every soldier kills a Master and he's the last of the Illuminati. See what he does about it.*

"What's in it for you? Why should you care if the world dies or even a hundred thousand people?" I grit my teeth. "You're Palmer."

*You're missing the point. I don't care about the world dying. I just think the Game itself is more fun than winning it. I think it's more fun that the world is here, dying on its own like some big rotten apple tree. Without Jehovah, the Illuminati would have taken over one day. They would have taken it over because the United States is rotting from within and the world with it. The walls against dictatorship are too costly to maintain. But it may take many more lifetimes. Until then, we play the Game.*

I suddenly want to spit. "So this is all about a policy disagreement. A fucking policy disagreement. And all along, I was thinking you were doing this because of some noble reason."

*No, that's why you're doing it, not me.*

"You're still not telling me something."

*I told you all I'm going to tell you, Chad. Now stop being a pussy.*

"I think you made all of this up and none of it's real. You were molested by this guy when you were little and you want him dead, so you fabricated this entire thing in your head."

*Oh, but you forget that it was your idea.*

"I was manipulated into having the idea, then."

*Now who's a paranoid?*

"Why did you have to kill Jenny?"

I'm shaking with sobs now, I can't stop crying, I'm about to completely lose it.

The truck is rattling as I continue to pick up speed. Up ahead is a traffic light, glowing red in the dark. The road splits there, left and right. Straight ahead is a guardrail and a wall of blackness that swallows up my headlights.

"Why did you do it?"

I can barely see the road through the waves of tears.

This is when I scream.

I keep screaming, my brain screaming with me, every atom of me screaming in unison.

Catharsis is like being reborn.

The red traffic light rushes towards me.

Beyond it, my headlights illuminate the gaunt shapes of trees.

I scream until I slump against the wheel, exhausted, and slam on the brakes. The tires screech as the truck races to a halt, fishtailing as it goes. The engine idles. I'm aware of darkness all around me, a stillness, and I feel alone. But I'm not ready to die yet. I want to say screw it, screw the world, but I can't.

Palmer's voice speaks quietly in my earpiece:

*I didn't kill her, Chad.*

I lean my forehead against the coolness of the steering wheel, crying for Jenny.

*Turn right here. Galt's house is just down the road.*

I say nothing.

*Turn right. Now.*

I just want to sleep.

*We're running out of time, Chad.*

I grit my teeth, shift the truck into gear and make the turn.

I don't know if anything is real anymore, but I decide to kill Galt because, for no other reason, I want to make somebody pay for Jenny.

# 20

I'm lying in a clump of bushes, facing the front door of the giant house. The rifle is resting on the bipod and the stock is pressed against my shoulder, which is starting to ache already from about fifteen minutes of waiting.

Emmet Galt is possibly one of two people and I have to kill both of them.

*You should be lying in the bushes about seventy-five yards from the front door.*

In one reality, Galt is a recluse billionaire—an eccentric, harmless bachelor who loves dogs and generously donates millions to charities and the arts each year.

*Do not hesitate. Shoot him in the head. If you get a follow-up tap to the chest, good.*

In another reality, Galt is the most powerful man in the world and leads a secret society that has been at war with the Catholic Church for two thousand years.

*Remember your training.*

The house is enormous, a mansion shaped as a quad, with a courtyard and a fountain. It's as big as a royal palace. All of the lights are on and I see dark figures moving in the windows. The outside of the house is lighted brilliantly from its foundation, casting tiny shadows across its surface that make the thousands of ornate details stand out in sharp relief.

*He should be coming out in less than ten minutes.*

A black limousine with tinted windows waits outside the court-yard, at the end of the long driveway, its engine idling. It pulled out of the stables about five minutes ago. Galt, Palmer told me, doesn't like using private helicopters. He prefers to be driven.

The time is 6:30 p.m.

I'm trembling from the cold and I have to pee.

Galt and I have one thing in common. Both of us are one of two people depending on what you believe. In one reality, I'm an unemployed mental health worker, your average nobody who gets a gun and goes postal. In another, I'm mankind's last hope.

Basically, if you believe one thing, then he's the nut, and if you believe the other, then I'm the nut. The truth is so obscure, I don't even know which reality is right. You might say I'm the nut but then I'd say, well, you really don't know for sure, do you.

*Remember not to hesitate. Simply take a breath, hold it, size up your target and squeeze the trigger. The act itself has no signifi-cance. It is just an act. Like tying your shoelaces.*

This part, what I'm seeing and doing right now, is all too true.

Light spills into the area I'm in from a neighboring property, which has a lot of landscape lighting in the garden on the other side of the wall. A little too much light for my liking, but then, I'm about seventy-five yards from the front of the house. I feel safe.

Men in black suits are walking around outside, talking casual-ly, one of them smoking.

This is the moment of truth, as they say.

Palmer's object of hatred might be the Grand Sovereign Master of the Illuminati, or it might be a man who molested him. Palmer might be completely insane, or he might not. Palmer might be trying to save the world, or he might not.

He taught me to be skeptical, to question everything, to be paranoid, and yet now I'm going to kill somebody on an act of pure faith. For a conspiracy theory.

What if the President getting shot was just a coincidence? Or what if the guy who shot Jackson was a friend of Palmer's? What if Jenny is still alive somewhere?

I realize that I'd rather believe that she is somewhere, happy, in the arms of another man, than dead. I still love her.

I put my thoughts about Jenny out of my head fast.

If I shoot this guy, nothing will happen. I'll probably never know if I prevented a germ from being released, or prevented this ancient secret society from taking over the world. The whole thing is still so ridiculous that it's both plausible and impossible, but not true. It does make an interesting theory, however.

What a mindfuck. And I have a feeling that it's not over yet.

Palmer seems to know what I'm thinking because I hear his voice in my ear.

*What if there is no God or a Heaven, says the atheist.*

*What if you die and find out there is a God and a Heaven, says the Christian.*

*The atheist converts.*

The front door of the house opens. The men around the front of the house stiffen, become more alert. Startled, I pull myself together and peer through my scope, setting the crosshairs on the bright light coming through the open doorway. A figure appears, but it's not him. Another bodyguard. Then another. Angry-looking whitebread boys wearing dark suits. The men in black. At last, Galt appears. My heart jumps. He pauses in the doorway, smiling at one of his cronies, sharing a joke. The light gleams on his glasses. He strolls down the steps and heads towards the car.

This man molested my brother, then killed my parents and my wife—or maybe he didn't.

I have six seconds, five, four.

It's time to kill this theory once and for all. I squeeze the trigger.

The bullet whines through the air and hits the man in the head, taking the top of his skull clean off. A spurt of blood shoots high into the air and he pitches back.

I squeeze the trigger, hitting him in the throat.

I squeeze the trigger, hitting him in the chest.

He goes down. He's dead.

Holy shit, I just killed him. I killed him.

The men in black are already heading towards me, holding small but powerful flashlights. Red laser target-finders shine from their automatic pistols.

I run as fast as I can, clawing my way to safety through the dense brush, my feet crashing through the dry leaves, and the noise I make only makes them run harder, giving them something to guide them right to me.

I hear the limousine roaring down the driveway.

The red lines of lasers wave through the branches, and I hear the science-fiction sound of automatic fire from weapons fitted with silencers. Bullets, a lot of bullets, whizz through the brush and crack off treebark. Dust, leaves, branches and little bits of wood fly all around me.

I drop to the ground, reload and turn on them. I size up the lead man, a silhouette against the blazing lights of the house, and fire. He drops.

I size up the next man, visible only by his flashlight and traces of his form, and fire again twice. The flashlight drops.

I get up, turn and run like hell through the dark, trying to trace the complicated route that Palmer had taken me to get here past the security cameras.

Suddenly the entire estate is lit up in bright light and an alarm bell is ringing. For a moment I'm blinded and simply stand there, stunned.

Security cameras are whirring everywhere, trying to target me, but I'm running along the shadow of a wall now, crouched low, looking for the hole I dug under it earlier.

"Chad," a voice hisses.

I freeze, then see Palmer waving at me from a clump of bushes nearby.

"Over here," he says.

I run to him, still crouched low, clutching the rifle.

"What are you doing here?"

"I came to help. I thought you were going to lose your mind and botch it. Sorry."

"He's dead, Palmer," I whisper.

"I'm going to get you out of here."

"I killed him. Now you have what you wanted. You can tell me the truth now."

Palmer is smiling in the shadows.

"Jeez, you never let up on me, Chad. Get ready for it."

"What?"

"The truth. Here it comes, any minute now. It'll make you feel a whole lot better. Trust me."

Just then, the lights go out. The alarm bells die off. The entire world hushes, grows quiet. The entire world, it seems, fades to black. Primordial darkness, turning back the clock more than a hundred years. The air is filled with distant sounds of a hundred cars honking and dogs barking. Overhead, the sky lights up with millions of stars.

The power has gone out over the entire eastern United States.

Inside thousands of homes, people are getting out their guns.

"The power's out," I say, filled with awe. "We're too late."

"Now you know it's true," he says. "Doesn't that make you feel better?"

•

It doesn't, actually. A hundred thousand people are going to die in this mess.

"Don't worry about it," Palmer says. "You saved the world, brother. That's what we wanted." He grins. "We won, brother. We beat them. That's the truth. Now let's get out of here."

"No tricks. It's really over now."

"Come on, or they'll find us."

He darts away from me, heading towards the hole I dug under the wall. I start to run after him, but my legs lock up and I fall, hitting the ground hard.

I'm lying on the ground, my eyes open and the right side of my head resting on the cold grass, and I can't move. I'm paralyzed. I can't even talk. All I can do is breathe, see and listen. I felt a tiny little sting when he hugged me, and now there's a drug inside me.

In the darkness, I hear Palmer's voice: "I just want you to know that I didn't lie to you. The Masters really were going to unleash a plague to finish the Game. You really did save the world. You should be proud."

This is the part where Palmer kills me so there will be no loose ends. This is something else I knew would happen but chose not to believe. Since I'm his brother, for some reason I thought I was safe.

Palmer says, "You've proven to yourself that one man truly can change the world, Chad. Forget one man, one vote. Make that one man, one bullet."

I hear a click as a bullet is loaded into the firing chamber of his pistol. My heart races as I realize that I am about to be shot in the head. I'm wondering if he's going to put the gun in my hand, make it look like a suicide.

At this moment, I know that everything he's told me is a lie. There is no Illuminati. There is simply Palmer, who is a psychopath on a mission of revenge against the man who turned him into one.

Then again, the power did go out. I want to puzzle this out, but I can't.

Instead, I'm thinking, this is the last moment of my life.

No, this one is.

No, this one is.

Palmer says, "The thing is, brother, that it doesn't mean the Illuminati has to end. All of us Princes. . . . Well, somebody has to take over and keep the Game going. We never really left them, you know. We were always Princes, mingling with the enemy, becoming their leaders, like wolves in sheep's clothes."

He laughs and draws close enough that I can feel his breath on my face.

"Jenny dying, losing your job, was all to isolate you and make you susceptible to paranoia. To turn you into the perfect assassin. Now you have the truth and the answers."

If I get out of this, I tell myself, I'm going to kill you. But I'm not getting out of this. Right now, realizing I'm about to die, I believe that life is not at all like a movie.

Palmer keeps talking close to my ear.

"I would have liked for you to have joined us, become a Prince yourself. I'm not kidding; I had it planned from the start that you would take my place as the new Simon Magus. But I can't trust you, Chad. You've got all the makings for a fine member of the Order, and this entire experience has brought you close to illumination, but you've got this ugly streak of morality that holds you back and makes you weak, tears you apart. You're simply too nice a guy. Killing you would be doing you a favor because you're doomed to be unhappy, always wanting but never getting what you want."

I hear other voices.

I'm wondering when Palmer is going to go ahead and shoot me before Galt's bodyguards come and kill him, too.

Palmer calls out, "I got him. Over here, Randy. Doug. Follow my voice."

Men are tramping through the bushes, holding flashlights, and suddenly they're standing around me. I catch a glimpse of black leather dress shoes before I'm blinded by the flashlights.

"You all right, Simon Magus?" one of them asks.

"Yeah, I'm fine. I caught him, stunned him with a dose of paralyzer."

"Is he *Soldati*?"

"Who knows."

"Yeah, he's a fucking Jezzie, look at him."

"He killed Spartacus."

"Where armies failed, one man achieved the death of the king."

"The Grail King is dead."

"He killed Olson and Ramsey. I just checked them and they're dead."

I can't even scream.

"This is one big fuckup."

I hear footsteps. "I just got off the phone!"

"The phone's out."

"I used a cell phone, stupid. Listen: The Masters are dead. All of them."

The voices curse in the dark. Feet shuffle.

Then the tone of the voices change.

"Simon Magus, you are in charge here now."

"Call him by his proper name, Callahan."

I'm thinking, I'm wrong. I'm very wrong.

There is an Illuminati.

"So what should we do with this Jezzie bastard?"

"We'll do what we always do."

I'm wetting myself right now.

"It'll be hard to do the ritual. We don't have any light. It'll be hell just finding the tools."

"I've got a pocketknife."

"Maybe we should just put a bullet in his head instead, right here."

I feel the barrel of a gun pressed hard against the side of my head, shoving my face into the grass.

This is the last moment of your life.

"Shall I do it, Spartacus?"

No, this one is.

This one.

It's at this point that the light is swallowed by a sea of colorful stars, which are swallowed by a void, total darkness.

# 21

**Billionaires Murdered in Mysterious Conspiracy**
by Ronald Pipes, *America Today*

PRINCETON, NEW JERSEY. *Moments before the severe power outage that plunged the entire east coast into a twelve-hour blackout, thirteen billionaires in eight states were murdered in what appeared to FBI investigators to be an elaborate conspiracy among some of the nation's foremost conspiracy theorists.*

*At approximately 6:40 pm EST on Sunday, thirteen men, among them five members of various Patriot and militia groups, murdered wealthy businessmen living in thirteen separate cities using sniper rifles and automatic pistols. The victims were gunned down as each left his home or hotel, where nine of them were staying in the New York area, at about the same time, according to witnesses. Bodyguards accompanying each of the victims returned fire and killed eleven of the assassins; in one gunbattle, two bodyguards were also shot dead.*

*All of the victims and the eleven assailants who were shot were pronounced dead on arrival, according to hospital spokespeople.*

*Two of the assassins were taken into custody by local police authorities, who on Sunday turned them over to the FBI, which is now heading the investigation.*

*The surviving assassins are Alan Mackey, 37, a resident of Mount Lebanon, New York, the owner and operator of a popular conspiracy-related web site, and Chad Carver, 34, a resident of Riverdale, New Jersey, an unemployed mental health worker.*

*Carver smirked at onlookers as he was led into the Princeton police department Monday morning, wearing a bulletproof vest. He was charged with conspiracy, multiple criminal homicide and reckless endangerment. Local police authorities reported that Carver killed three people during a brief exchange of fire.*

*Officials at the Justice Department said that under the Comprehensive Anti-Terrorism Act of 1995, Carver and Mackey's crime may be considered a capital offense by the courts should the murders be regarded as politically motivated.*

*Among the victims were men living in cities as different as Chicago and New York, Philadelphia and San Francisco, who were all in the New York area that night, either at their homes or in local hotels. They shared several other common traits. All were worth more than thirty billion dollars, were socially recluse, had no families and were quiet philanthropists and patrons of the arts. All served on various boards of directors of many of the same Fortune 500 companies, and received substantial income from consulting fees.*

*Although hampered by the effects of the blackout and with resources strained in helping local police to suppress the looting and rioting that occurred, the FBI worked with hospital authorities to identify the bodies of nine of the other assassins and discovered that virtually all of them had ties to militia, Patriot and other groups obsessed with conspiracy theories. The two exceptions are Kevin McClellan, 36, a former patient at Mercer County Psychiatric Hospital in Trenton, New Jersey, and Carver, who worked as an orderly at the hospital up until one week before the shootings.*

*So far, however, the FBI refused to comment on the motive for the killings or if they are connected with the blackout, the cause of which is still puzzling investigators. White House officials said*

*that the death toll of the blackout is now fourteen hundred and
rising.*

*"We are conducting a vigorous investigation to gather evi-
dence, determine the motive for the shootings, and probe the suspects to learn the scope and methods behind the murders," said
FBI Director Marshal Lions. "We are convinced at this stage,
due to the coordinated nature of the attacks, that this was the
result of elaborate planning by the perpetrators. Further, we have
ample reason to believe that these crimes were perpetrated under
the direction or with the cooperation of others as of yet unidenti-
fied."*

*He said that several of the perpetrators had received large
sums of money deposited in their savings accounts over the past
six days from a Swiss bank. He also said that how the conspirators received their weapons remains, at present, a mystery, pointing to a larger conspiracy, prompting further investigation by the
FBI.*

*Lions said that so far, however, a search of all the suspects'
houses had turned up nothing except dozens of printed pages of
mysterious encrypted messages posted on web site bulletin
boards and transmitted through e-mail.*

*Lions said that the FBI did discover, however, that in the morn-
ing hours just after the blackout ended, Jenny Carver, 32, wife of
Chad Carver, was found dead in her car, which was half-sub-
merged in a pond near Arlington, Virginia. Local authorities
reported that she had been dead for more than ten days and that
she had died of heart failure, although an autopsy is pending to
confirm this initial assessment.*

*Martin Dobbs, Carver's supervisor at Mercer County
Psychiatric Hospital, said he told the FBI that Carver was a
"good man, always willing to help," but had lately become dis-
traught, calling in sick at work repeatedly up until he was laid off
due to county budget cutbacks.*

*Others close to Carver told* America Today *that he was
"upstanding," "always willing to help," "quiet and thoughtful,"*

*and expressed shock and disbelief that he participated in the murders. All of them said that he had never shown a belief in conspiracy theories.*

*Lions refused to reveal any statements that Carver and Mackey might have made to the FBI, although sources close to the investigation said that although the men did not know each other, they were both aware of the same plan to carry out the attacks; both had a "controller" who directed their actions; and both believed that all of the victims were involved in a conspiracy to overthrow the U.S. government.*

*"Whether the perpetrators acted on an irrational common belief or some other reason, we cannot be sure at this time," said Lions. "We are still looking for a reasonable motive as well as further direct evidence of an organization."*

*According to Carver and Mackey, the victims were planning to unleash a biological weapon, which would wipe out billions of people across the earth, then exploit the resulting collapse of the United States as a means to take over the government.*

*"All of the men involved appeared to communicate with each other using heavily encrypted messages on web site bulletin boards and e-mails," said Lions, adding, "On the surface, the communications appear to focus on the death of Princess Diana, which occurred more than ten years ago, and common chain letters. We have not as of yet been able to crack the cipher or the code."*

*A further hamper to what is already a complex investigation is that Mackey is suffering from severe lymphatic, bone and bowel cancer and is under heavy medication, limiting the FBI's ability to question him.*

*Conspiracy theorists are individuals who regard the government with suspicion and look for connections between world events to find sinister evidence of conspiracy. For years, they have operated at the fringe of American society, giving dire warnings of an imminent takeover by an invisible government. Most of their activities involve researching and sharing informa-*

*tion in published form and over the Internet. Others have translated their beliefs into action, such as forming paramilitary groups and training in military weapons and tactics to resist a perceived imminent takeover of the government. All of them have warned America time and time again of secret societies, private meetings, surveillance by the authorities, and assassinations.*

*"These people wanted a conspiracy, and they finally got one, a big one, of their own conception, design and execution," said Lions.*

*He added, "We have reason to believe that this conspiracy reaches farther into the dark underworld of conspiracy theorists and other extremists," promising a probe into all conspiracy-related groups during its continuing investigation of the murders.*

*According to an* America Today *poll conducted last spring, 6.7% percent of American adults aged 18 and over profess a serious belief in various conspiracy theories and 57.2% admit a mild belief. In the same poll, 53% said they believed, for example, that President John F. Kennedy was murdered by a conspiracy in 1963.*

*Today, more than 20,000 Americans belong to the Liberty Lobby; more than 50,000 belong to the John Birch Society; and more than 20,000 belong to various Neo-Nazi and white supremacy groups. More than 220 armed militias and 500 Patriot groups are currently operating in the United States.*

# 22

Excerpts from "www.GrandConspiracy.com Message Board"

Consiranoia Message Board
Cover-ups and Conspiracies

Joyous Mistrust is a sign of health.
—Friedrich Nietzsche

Reply Add Thread View By Thread

Search | Send to a Friend | Help < Prev M | Next M >

Xena_Heartslayer                          1:13 a.m.
Assassination Conspiracy - The joke's on us
*Well folks it was definitely strange to see a real-live conspiracy unfold right before our eyes on tv among all the wreckage of the big blackout - perpetrated by some of the country's biggest conspiracy theorists - looks like the joke's on us... \*s\* i believe in keeping an eye out for what the government's doing but killing anonymous rich men is not the answer - now the governmetn is really going to come down on our heads - sleep well - especially you, chemtrailer, take care ;-) - peace out - Xena :-)*

CloseEncounter3                              1:27 a.m.
Re:Assassination Conspiracy - The joke's on us

*I've been burning the midnight oil tonight reading about what Carver and Mackey et al did and I can't believe it ... this whole thing reeks of a set-up ... I hear they're going to submit Carver to a polygraph but not Mackey cuz Mackey is going to be dead within a week from the looks of it ... his doctor said that he didn't have cancer as of a month before the killings and that he's puzzled ... cancer that kills you in a week, hmmmm... I think you're right Xena the joke really is on us because we're being fed a real mind-job for exmaple where did they get the rifles that they used to kill those old gyus? I think maybe Carver and Mackey were onto something & did what they did and now it's being spun like they're a bunch of crazies ... they musta targeted those thirteen men for a reason don't you think? I wonder what guns they'll ban because of this ... I'm also curious about that weird Princess Diana connection that Lions was talking about ... I'm sitting here wondering if the murders have anythig to do with Jackson getting shot and Dr. Hiram Gaines disappearing off the face of hte earth and of course the Power Outage that killed so many people and showed all of us just how powerful the police can be in times of crisis, I mean did you see those freakin tanks? Anyhow, the timing is eerie. I think there are connections between all of these events that need to be explored when we get over our collective shock. We should keep looking into it I thik there's more in all this than meets the all-seeing eye - ttfn —CloseEncounter*

Baphomet                                     1:38 a.m.
Re:Assassination Conspiracy - The joke's on us
*Jacques de Molay, thou art avenged!*

jedgarhoover                                  1:56 a.m.
Re:Assassination Conspiracy - The joke's on us
*Carver's belief in conspiracies may get him off as a mental case otherwise it's technically terorism what he did and he could*

*fry for it under the law. The stuff he told the FBI had a ring of truth to it even though it was the wildest conspiracy theory I ever heard then again the FBI hasn't told us everything just a little of what Carver told them! Nobody but the FBI has the full story (oh, sh\*t). The little the FBI reported that he said makes sense in a way and is worth looking into. Did anybody else hear about Richard Matherson's (one of the rich guys who got shot) CIA connections? I agree iwth Close Encounter that Carver and Mackey were on to them for SOMETHIGN and it had to be big! Maybe like Close Enounter said it had something to do with the prez getting shot and the power going out on the eastern seaboard. A friend of mine lives out east in South Carolina and one of his neighbors got shot by National Guard while the power was out. F\*ck that was scary seeing the army on the streets, kind of a sneak preview for the poilce state that's coming! The whole country's falling apart it seems like. That sound you hear is the sh\*t hitting the fan. I think in the end we're going to find out that they were heroes and saved us from something we just don't know what yet. I started a member page about this conpsiracy here at www.GrandConspiracy.com devoted to the prez and blackout and disappearance of Hiram Gaines and ten other well-known con-spiracy experts! Keep the faith...remember, "the object of the game is to guess what the game is!"*

*P.S. any of you govt ppl coming to this site and keeping an eye on us just remember we're looking back!*

paranoidandroid                          2:13 a.m.
Re:Assassination Conspiracy - The joke's on us
*did anybody else see president croshaw on the tv talking about the crisis? he is one freaky looking dude. anybody else here think that he's an agent for the illuminati?*

studio_51                                2:40 a.m.
Re:Assassination Conspiracy - The joke's on us
*jeez, what the hell is wrong with you you guys got it all wrong.*

*the gvt and mythical illuminati had nothing to do with this. we should be looking into the conspirators themselves. f\*ck, we're conspiracy theorists and we're sitting here ignoring a big conspiracy right in our own community. everybody needs to get their heads out of their \*ss and stop pointing the finger at the gvt and instead look in a big mirror at ourselves. the fbi has conclusive evidence that the conspiracy was bigger than these 13 wackos. who else among us was in on it? that's what i'd like to know. — studio_51*

Jester                                                              2:49 a.m.
Re:Assassination Conspiracy - The joke's on us
*Do you work for the government, Studio 51?*

Spartacus                                                          3:15 a.m.
Re:Assassination Conspiracy - The joke's on us
*I will tell what really happened. Chad Carver, Alan Mackey and the eleven conspirators who died were part of an anti-illuminati group. They sought to kill the thirteen Grand Masters of the Illuminati to prevent this ancient organization from imposing The New World Order of America—in fact, to silence forever its satanic voice in history*

*What they did not know is that they were dupes for the illuminati themselves. Carver, Mackey and the rest were dupes of various generals and princes in the true Illuminati who wanted to kill their masters and take over the Illuminati for their own ends. These princes and generals worked directly for the thirteen Grand Masters of the Illuminati. Carver, Mackey and the rest killed the Grand Masters of the Illuminati as the dupes of these generals and princes so that these generals and princes could seize power for themselves. They were unwittingly helped by forces inside the Vatican. They are not criminals and should be given medals even though they ultimately failed their mission*

*The entire operation was a coup d'etat inside the Illuminati while we sat back and did nothing*

*Carver and Mackey escaped the bullet that was supposed to silence them forever but who knows for how long. Mackey was injected with fast-acting cancer so he is dying. Carver is in a mental hospital. He probably won't last long there either. He told the FBI, CIA, NSA and the IRS the truth but nobody is believing him*

*The Masters were going to release a biological weapon called Jehovah on all mankind while they waited it out in underground bases. The generals and princes did not like that because they had it too good. They did not want Jehovah unleashed so they made a conspiracy inside the conspiracy and killed the Masters then took their place. This is after the Masters shot President Jackson and cut off the power on the East Coast to create chaos*

*This is all true—every word of it*

*This I also know to be true:*

*That which is above is like that which is below and that which is below is like that which is above*

*Think about it*

*I am posting this message on every conspiracy message board to get the truth out about what really happened. Tell everybody you know about the truth and write to your Congressman.* Ordo ab Chaos—*Out of Chaos Comes Order*—Spartacus

Printed in the United States
33281LVS00002B/382-402